"You and I had a good thing once."

Lucy turned back to the horizon. As soon as she broke eye contact, he ached for it again.

It was every man's fantasy to have his first love admit she still thought of him, but he wasn't prepared for the pain of actually hearing the words.

"We were kids," he said. "Neither of us knew what we were doing or where we were going. I won't deny what I felt for you was real, but as much as I'd love to go back in time, we're not those people anymore."

"I'd like to think we're better."

"I'll give you that." He reached for her hand and gave it a gentle squeeze.

The instant he touched her, Lane knew he shouldn't have come. He needed to get back in his truck and leave her and the past alone before his heart paid the price a second time...

Dear Reader,

This book was never part of my original plan. The day I finished writing *Mistletoe Rodeo* was a bittersweet one. I felt accomplished that I'd completed the Ramblewood series, but a part of me felt as if I'd walked away from the people I loved. Three months passed and I still couldn't shake the feeling. My mom and I discussed it one afternoon over coffee and she nudged me to continue the series. I outlined *The Trouble with Cowgirls* that evening.

I'd always wanted to delve deeper into the Travisonno family. We'd met Nicolino throughout many of the previous books, and his history as an Italian immigrant on a Texas horse ranch had always intrigued me. This was my chance to tell part of his story.

Nicolino and Lucy pay homage to my own family. My grandfather's middle name was Nicolino and one of his sisters was Lucy. As with my other books, I've woven some more of my own ancestral elements into Ramblewood.

The Trouble with Cowgirls is the seventh book in the Welcome to Ramblewood series...where the door is always open.

Please visit me at amandarenee.com. I'd love to hear from you. Happy reading!

Amanda Renee

THE TROUBLE WITH COWGIRLS

—

AMANDA RENEE

HARLEQUIN® AMERICAN ROMANCE®

Recycling programs
for this product may
not exist in your area.

ISBN-13: 978-0-373-75624-7

The Trouble with Cowgirls

Printed in U.S.A.

www.Harlequin.com

Amanda Renee was raised in the northeast and now wriggles her toes in the warm sand of coastal South Carolina. Her career began when she was discovered through Harlequin's So You Think You Can Write contest. When not creating stories about love and laughter, she enjoys the company of her schnoodle, Duffy, camping, playing guitar and piano, photography, and anything involving horses. You can visit her at amandarenee.com.

Books by Amanda Renee

Harlequin American Romance

Welcome to Ramblewood

Betting on Texas
Home to the Cowboy
Blame It on the Rodeo
A Texan for Hire
Back to Texas
Mistletoe Rodeo

Visit the Author Profile page
at Harlequin.com for more titles.

For Mom

Thank you for always encouraging me

I love you always

Chapter One

"I want to go home."

Lucy Travisonno tightened her grip on Carina's little hand as they stepped out of her cousin Nicolino's truck into the mid-afternoon Texas sun. Dust from the dirt drive churned behind them. Her eight-and-a-half-year-old daughter's words echoed her own thoughts. The town of Ramblewood had been a reprieve from her overly strict Italian family since she was fourteen. And while she might have dreamed of visiting the Bridle Dance Ranch again one day, she'd never imagined returning out of desperation.

Ella, Nicolino's wife, waved to them from the front porch of their sun-shower yellow Queen Anne farmhouse. Five children barreled down the steps toward them, causing Carina to tuck herself behind Lucy. Even though the children were Texas born, each of them greeted Lucy and Carina in Italian while shaking their hands.

"It's wonderful to see you. I can't believe it's been ten years." Ella's melodious Southern drawl and welcoming embrace warmly enveloped Lucy. "Let me get a good look at you." Ella withdrew, holding her at arm's length. "Still as pretty as ever. How are you holding up, honey?"

"We're surviving." Lucy guardedly observed her daughter's reactions to her new second cousins and then lowered her voice. "Carina's having trouble accepting all of this and I feel like I'm failing as a parent."

"My heart aches for the both of you." Ella smothered her with another hug. "I can't even imagine what you've been through, but you're with family now and we'll take good care of you."

"Thank you." Ella's compassion intensified the pressure welling in Lucy's chest. Her divorce from Antonio had been difficult enough for their daughter to accept, but his death had left Carina inconsolable. "That means the world to me. I don't know if she'll ever get past losing her father."

"She will in time. Moving from Italy to Texas is a big adjustment. And just so you know, we only told the children about Antonio's death." Ella squeezed her hand. "We didn't feel the rest was theirs or anyone else's concern."

The past few months had been a nightmare for Lucy, but they'd been hardest for Carina. Antonio had been so deep in debt at the time of his death that everything they'd owned had been seized shortly afterward—including their daughter's beloved horses. Lucy hoped Carina would begin to heal now that they'd moved away from the constant reminders of what they'd lost.

"I appreciate Nicolino giving me this job opportunity and your aunt Kay's generosity in renting us one of the cottages until we're back on our feet. I was a bit of a troublemaker when I used to visit. I'm surprised she's allowing me to stay on the ranch."

"You were a cakewalk compared to her boys. Believe me—we're all happy you're here. Would you like to come in and have some sweet tea or a cup of coffee?"

Lucy glanced at her daughter, who couldn't have looked more miserable if she tried. "Would you mind if we passed? I feel grungy. We've been traveling for over twenty-four hours and I'm anxious to show Carina our new home."

"Of course." Ella smiled down at the little girl. "She's the spitting image of you. Give me one second and I'll get you the keys to the cottage."

Lucy brushed the hair from Carina's face. "How are you doing, *mia gattina*?" She'd affectionately called her daughter *my kitten* since the day she was born. Three months premature, Carina had never cried loudly as a baby. It was always more of a mew.

"I can't understand them," Carina said in Italian. "They don't speak much Italian and their English doesn't sound like the English I know."

Lucy had feared her daughter's thick accent compared to everyone else's Texas twang would make conversation difficult at first. "Give it a chance. Before you know it, you'll understand everything they're saying. The more you speak English, the easier it will become."

"I don't want to be here, Mamma." Carina pushed away, continuing in Italian, "This is your family. I want to go back to our house and my friends."

Lucy's stomach knotted. "Sweetheart, you know we can't do that. None of those things belong to us anymore and this is very much your family, too."

"Why did Papà have to die?" She folded her arms tightly across her chest—her walls up once again. The pain reflected in Carina's eyes gutted Lucy. Her fun-loving daughter hadn't laughed or smiled since before Antonio's death. Now, four months later, she appeared harder and much older.

Ella returned with multiple keys and handed them to Lucy. "This is for the cottage, this one's for our house in case you ever need something and we're not home and this last one is for my car. I'm not using it, since Nicolino bought me an SUV, so please take it for as long as you need."

"Thank you, Ella." Lucy fought back the tears that threatened to break free. She'd managed to remain strong for Carina's sake and refused to show any weakness now.

"Follow me over to your place and then I'll leave you be. Do promise to join us for dinner tonight. I've stocked your kitchen, but we planned a small gathering to welcome you to Texas."

"We wouldn't miss it," Lucy answered for the two of them, knowing Carina wanted nothing to do with it. She also had the feeling Ella and Nicolino had prepared a feast rather than an intimate family meal.

After Ella had shown them around the cottage and

left, they were alone for the first time since they'd departed Italy. Carina's brows lifted in anticipation of Lucy's next words.

"I know you were hoping for more, but this is the best I can do." It had taken every penny to send ahead what belongings they had left and to pay for their plane tickets and the bare necessities. "I promise you, we will get through this together."

Carina didn't argue; she didn't cry; she didn't say a word, and it had become increasingly frustrating. Lucy wanted to help her daughter, but she no longer knew how. Antonio had been Carina's confidant, and that had suited Lucy just fine. She'd wanted them to maintain a close relationship. Even after the divorce, which had been amicable, Antonio had made a point to see Carina almost every day. He'd been the one helping her with her homework while Lucy earned her master's degree. He'd also been her dressage instructor, grooming her to be a champion one day. When he died, Carina's dreams had died with him. And there was no convincing her that it was all right to continue pursuing those dreams in memory of her father.

Lucy glanced around the tiny two-bedroom cottage. Okay, so it was a long way from their eighteenth-century luxury villa in Parma, but the house was cozy, and for the first time in months she felt secure. Worn oak planks replaced the marble-and-parquet flooring they were accustomed to. There were Sheetrock ceilings above instead of ornate coffered ones and rustic hand-me-downs in place of her elegant furnishings.

The cottage was tidy and freshly painted inside and out. Ella had taken care to add personal touches such as handmade quilts and family heirlooms that Lucy suspected were special to her and Nicolino. Outside, freshly mulched beds filled with vibrant late-summer flowers lined both sides of the front walkway. The strawberry-colored cottage with its white trim was quaint and inviting. No, it wasn't luxurious, but it was clean, and more important…it was theirs.

"This is what they call shabby chic." She knew Carina had already popped in her iPod earbuds and drowned out her words, but Lucy feared if she stopped moving or talking, she'd think about the last time she was in Ramblewood.

"It's in the past." Lucy dragged her suitcases into the bedroom. "And it needs to stay there."

They might have lost almost everything they'd owned, but Ramblewood was their chance at a fresh start, and she'd do whatever it took to ensure it was successful. The sooner she and Carina developed a new routine, the sooner they'd rebuild their lives and their relationship. After dinner she'd insist on starting her new job tomorrow. Nicolino would understand. Having emigrated from Italy to Texas almost twenty-five years ago, he'd begun a new life on this very ranch and worked his way up to general operations manager. Now it was her turn, and Lucy refused to allow anything to get in the way.

LANE MORGAN LEFT the bunkhouse before sunrise. He could barely contain his excitement as he made his way to the Bridle Dance Ranch stables. The rumor was Nicolino Travisonno had gathered many of the ranch employees to announce Lane's long-awaited promotion to barn manager. He'd known the day was coming, but he hadn't expected this much fanfare.

He had worked beside the last barn manager on the quarter-of-a-million-acre paint and cutting horse ranch since he was a teenager. An after-school job had turned full time once he'd graduated high school. When Curly had announced his retirement last month, Lane had expected Nicolino to offer him the position then. Curly's last day had come and gone over three weeks ago, and Lane continued to wait. He'd been doing Curly's job ever since and at this point an official announcement was only a formality.

"Today's the day." A ranch hand slapped him on the back. "You deserve it."

That he did. Lane hadn't been fortunate enough to attend college full time the way many of his friends had, but he'd managed to take night classes as time permitted. At twenty-eight, he still had another two years to go until he earned his bachelor's degree, and he was determined to do it. Curly wasn't college educated, but he'd been the best barn manager anyone could've hoped for. Lane had apprenticed under the man, studying everything equine and stable related he could find. Curly had groomed him for this promotion, and Lane was confident it was his.

Along with everyone else, Lane filed into the

country French stone and stucco stables. The building had been nicknamed the Horse Mansion due to its rivaling the size of a football field.

"May I have everyone's attention, please?" Nicolino's voice boomed as the crowd converged in the timber-framed center area. They quieted down, leaving only the sound of an occasional horse neigh to break the electrified silence. "As you're all aware, Curly's retirement left a vacancy in the barn manager position."

The hair on the back of Lane's neck rose in anticipation. He heard somebody whisper "Good luck" behind him. Nodding silently, he focused his attention on Nicolino.

"Today I'm proud to award the position to Lucy Travisonno."

"Who?" someone called out from the other side of the room.

Lane lifted his eyes to the front of the crowd. He swore his heart stopped beating at the sight of her. His first love and the woman who'd vanished from his life without so much as a word.

Time had treated her well. She was more beautiful than he remembered—her light olive complexion appeared illuminated by the morning sunlight filtering in from above through the large Craftsman-style windows. Her hazel-green eyes met his and for a brief moment he thought he saw her waver, as though she was as surprised to see him as he was to see her. Quickly recovering, she squared her shoulders and looked at her attentive audience. She'd always had the ability to captivate people.

"I'm very excited to be here and I look forward to meeting every one of you." Lucy scanned the room, but seemed to avoid the area where he stood. "When you see me around, please say hello and introduce yourself. But be patient—there are a lot of you and I'm not always great with remembering names. Although I do recognize some of you from many years ago."

Lane wasn't sure which to react to—the fact that Lucy was back in town or that she'd stolen his promotion. At the very least, Nicolino could have told him privately. He of all people knew how this would affect him. The sound of everyone talking at once roared in his ears.

Lucy stepped down from the small raised area and Nicolino began speaking again. Lane couldn't concentrate on the words. He needed fresh air.

Outside, he took a few deep breaths. Most people knew when to avoid him and this was definitely one of those times. As everyone filed out of the stables, a few glanced his way, but most steered clear. When he saw Nicolino, he quickly caught up to the man.

"What gives?" Lane demanded. The ranch hands and grooms within listening distance turned toward them.

"Not here." Nicolino motioned to the small outdoor stable office near the main corral. Following him inside, Nicolino closed the door. "I know you're surprised to see Lucy again."

Lane snorted. "Well, there's that and the fact you gave your cousin my promotion. What experience does she have?"

"Lane." Nicolino held up his hands. "It was never your promotion. I considered you as a candidate and I decided on Lucy. I applaud your enthusiasm and continuing your education, but I have to put this business first. I'm sorry, but you don't have the skill set it takes to be barn manager of a ranch this size. Lucy does. She has a master's degree in equine science and will probably earn her doctorate in the near future. You can learn a lot from her, providing you put what happened between you two in the past."

Lane's shoulders slumped as he attempted to digest Nicolino's words. The last he'd seen of Lucy, she'd been a party girl with absolutely no direction in life. The little she knew about horses back then had come from what he'd taught her during the summers on the ranch. He'd worked with horses all his life and had been her teacher. How could she be better suited for the job than him?

"It shouldn't just be about education. Practical experience should carry more weight." Lane's jaw tightened. "You knew all along you would never promote me to barn manager, didn't you?"

Nicolino lowered his eyes and rubbed the back of his neck. "When Curly announced his retirement, I immediately thought the job would be perfect for Lucy. That's not to say I hadn't considered you, too. And before you say it—no, I didn't choose Lucy because she's family. I chose her because she's better qualified."

Lane's stomach hardened. Curly had announced his retirement six weeks ago. All this time he'd thought the position had been his. "You could have told me at any point between then and now. Letting me find out in front of everyone was cruel. I know you've never been my biggest fan. You made that clear when I dated Lucy ten years ago and you've never let me forget it, but a little respect would've been appreciated."

"You're right." Nicolino nodded. "I knew how much you wanted it and I should've told you. It has nothing to do with you once dating Lucy—it was strictly a business decision. That being said, I'm sure I don't have to remind you that she's your new boss. You're an excellent employee and I need you here, but if working with her is going to be a problem, you may want to start looking elsewhere. Lucy's here to stay."

Nicolino's words punched him in the gut. He could work for a woman. He could even work for Lucy, but he didn't feel he should have to. Nicolino was wrong. He was qualified to manage Bridle Dance and he'd prove it.

"Understood." Lane left the office and headed for the stables where he'd last seen Lucy. Their reunion had been a long time coming and Lane wished it were in a private setting instead of the middle of his workplace. Spotting her halfway up the spiral staircase leading to the main administrative offices, Lane called out to her.

"Lucy, do you have a minute?"

She froze at the sound of his voice, not turning to face him at first. Slowly she loosened her white-knuckled grip on the railing and made her way back down the stairs.

"Lane, I'm surprised to see you. I thought you had moved to Wyoming."

Her Italian accent wasn't as heavy as he remembered. Her English had improved significantly, but her voice was still velvety rich and deep, yet utterly feminine.

He had waited ten years to have this conversation, and the resentment he'd bottled up finally broke free. "I was in Wyoming. Waiting for you in the apartment that I'd rented for us. But you never came." He could taste the bitterness in his tone. "You never answered any of my calls or emails. Then, a year later, I found out you'd gone and married someone else. So I guess you could say I never thought I'd see you again."

"Lower your voice, please. If you want to discuss this, we will, but my employees don't need to know my personal business."

"Your employees." Lane smirked. "How easily the phrase rolls off your tongue. For the record, I'm one of your employees. I'm sure there are quite a few around here who remember you, and many others probably already know we dated for four years."

"We were teenagers back then, and what do you mean you work for me?" Lucy asked.

"I'm your second-in-command—the assistant barn manager."

"I didn't know." Lucy squeezed her eyes shut and for a moment Lane wondered if she was attempting to wish him away. She opened them and came a step closer. "Things got complicated after I left." Her voice was low. "I never meant to hurt you, but it's in the past. I'm trusting that we can work together, because, Lane, I could really use a friend right now. Someday I'll tell you all about it—but not today, and definitely not here. If you will please excuse me, I have paperwork to fill out upstairs. I'd like to meet with you later this afternoon to go over the barn schedules... if you have time."

Lucy's raw honesty startled him and Lane suspected that whatever had happened back then paled in comparison to what had happened recently. And that bothered him more than he cared to admit. "I'll be here. Page me if you can't find me."

"Mamma," a small voice called out from behind them.

"Carina!" Lucy perked up at the sight of the child, who was accompanied by Ella.

Lucy has a daughter?

"Did you come to see where I work?"

Carina nodded and quickly walked past her mother to the stalls. *"Sono molto belli!"*

"In English, Carina," Lucy corrected.

"They are very beautiful." The girl's thick accent was reminiscent of the one Lucy had had when they first met.

"Come here, *mia gattina*. I want you to meet someone." Lucy waved the girl over. "Lane, I would like to introduce you to my daughter, Carina."

"It's a pleasure to meet you." Lane shook her hand. His mind raced as he attempted to determine the girl's age. Finally, he asked, "How old are you?"

"Almost nine," she answered.

Lane swallowed hard, quickly doing the math in his head. He blew out a breath, relieved she couldn't possibly be his. When he looked up at Lucy, she shook her head and quickly looked away as if she'd read his mind.

"I'm going to show Carina around," Ella interrupted. "Then we'll head over to Aunt Kay's house."

Lucy gave her daughter a quick kiss goodbye. "Thank you, Ella." A silent look of concern briefly passed between the two women.

He waited until Carina was out of earshot before he attempted to explain. "I didn't mean to imply—"

"Yes, you did." Lucy brushed past him. "Your poker game must really suck with tells like those. You and I are in the past. Things happened, and we've both moved on, so let's not make a scene."

Things. Lane had thought they were more than a *thing* back then. "No problem." Lucy continued up the stairs as Lane watched Ella and Carina exit the stables. He felt like a damned fool. It had been bad enough finding out she'd married someone else. It was entirely different to know that while he'd been planning their future in Wyoming, Lucy had been carrying another man's baby. All the scenarios he'd imagined as to why he'd never heard from her again had always been forgivable. This wasn't.

Chapter Two

By lunchtime Lucy couldn't get out of work fast enough. Her first day wasn't exactly going as planned. The safety of her car provided little shelter against the torrent of emotions rocketing through her veins. Why hadn't Nicolino forewarned her about Lane?

When she was a teenager, she couldn't wait for the school year to end. Summers had meant seeing Lane again. From the moment her plane landed, they'd been inseparable whenever he wasn't working. By the end of their final summer together, he'd accepted a better job in Wyoming and they'd begun making plans to live there once Lucy had graduated from higher secondary school the following year. Their plans had been short-lived. Once Lucy arrived home in Italy, she'd discovered she was two months pregnant. Obviously she had been wrong in assuming Lane had stayed in Wyoming, but Nicolino should have mentioned it in conversation at some point.

She lowered the window in a desperate attempt to pull more air into her lungs. Tears clouded her vision at the memories of what could have been. Her fingers lightly brushed along the side of her rib cage. Underneath her shirt, inked into her skin for eternity was one word: Lane.

"I don't have time for this." Lucy started the ignition. Everything she did, despite Carina's protests, was for her daughter. There wasn't room for the past. Any efforts to push Lane to the back of her mind would probably prove futile, but for sanity's sake, she had to try. She had less than fifteen minutes to make her appointment to register Carina for school. Ella had offered to drive, but the school was close enough to find on her own. Besides, she was desperate for some much-needed alone time, however brief.

Carina had been out of school for only a little over a week, which was good considering their transcontinental move. The Texas school year had begun a week earlier, so Carina wouldn't be too far behind. Lucy pulled into the parking lot with seconds to spare. She was the school's first impression of her daughter and she didn't want to ruin it. Within an hour, she was on her way back to work. Overall, the enrollment had been painless enough because she'd emailed most of the paperwork before they'd left Italy.

The school's biggest concern was Carina's ability to speak English, despite Lucy's reassurance that her daughter was fluent in Italian, French and English. Now she wondered how well her daughter would do, given the way Carina had struggled to understand the language yesterday. Lucy had gone through the same learning curve during her first summer in America. But she'd only been vacationing and no one had expected her to understand perfectly. It would be different for Carina. Lucy couldn't sit beside her in school to make sure she grasped everything the teachers said, let alone translate the other students' slang on the playground. The additional change from private to public school had given her daughter one more reason not to talk to her. She'd heard other parents say the teenage years were the most unpleasant. If they were any worse than this, Lucy didn't think she'd survive. Hopefully, she could prepare herself over the next four years.

She pulled up beside Bridle Dance's main house. Ella's deceased uncle, Joe Langtry, had lovingly built the log mansion. Lucy had been heartbroken to hear of his passing four summers ago. He'd always gone out of his way to explain things to her, as had Lane. Lucy winced at how easily he came to mind and how much it still hurt to think about him. She needed to keep Lane out of her thoughts unless it was work related. She was his boss and anything else would be unprofessional, not that she wanted anything else to happen.

Seeing Ella in the Langtrys' side yard, Lucy stepped from the car.

"How did it go?" Ella unlatched the gate and held it open.

"Good. I'm a little concerned about the language issue, but I'm hopeful." She waved to Carina on the far side of the garden, but her daughter was too preoccupied with a large black poodle to even notice she was there. "How has she been?"

"Quiet." Ella smiled. "The most I've heard her talk is to the horses and Barney over there—and that was in Italian."

Lucy shrugged. "I guess there's no harm in it as long as she speaks English to other kids and her teachers. Are you sure you don't mind taking her clothes shopping today? I can take her after work."

"It's not a problem at all. My kids will take the bus home and keep themselves occupied until dinner." Ella's face brightened. "I'm looking forward to shopping with just one child for a change. It'll bring back memories of when I used to take you shopping."

Lucy appreciated Ella's offer to take Carina for school clothes. The local kids had picked on Lucy during her first summer in town and she didn't want her daughter to suffer the same fate. Italian fashions and Texas casual weren't exactly the same thing. Ella—who was fifteen years older than Lucy—had given her a Southern makeover back then and was bestowing the same kindness on Carina.

Lucy removed a small envelope of cash from her bag and handed it to Ella. "It's not much, but there should be enough in there for whatever she needs, within reason. I was thinking a few pieces to dress down what she already owns." Lucy hated to admit it, but she was glad Ella was the one taking Carina shopping. Her daughter wasn't as crabby with other people. "She won't be happy about going to a discount clothing store, but a lesson in frugality will do her some good. Besides, she's always hated wearing a school uniform, so this will give her the chance to play around and develop her own style." Lucy checked her watch. "I've been gone too long. I need to get back to work."

"Yes, you do," Nicolino said from behind her.

Lucy spun to face him. She might have held it together inside the stables, but outside, the gloves came off. "Why didn't you tell me Lane still worked here?"

Nicolino jammed his hands into his pockets. "If I had, would you have still taken the position?"

Lucy shook her head. The thought of Lane working there hadn't even entered her mind when Nicolino had offered her the job. "Maybe. I would have had to really think about it."

"Well, there you have it." Nicolino tilted his hat back, a bit too self-assured for Lucy's liking. "Under the circumstances, moving here was the best thing for you and Carina. I didn't want to risk you turning me down based on an old relationship."

"You know it was more than that." Lucy didn't want to remember how ashamed her parents had been of her when they'd learned she was pregnant with Lane's baby. "Enlighten me on one thing. Lane said he waited for me in Wyoming for a year before he found out I'd gotten married. But I married Antonio before Lane even left for Wyoming, and I asked you to tell him we were over."

"It wasn't my place to explain it to him, and since he was leaving, I didn't see the harm in keeping quiet. Never mind the fact that I wasn't too pleased he knocked up my baby cousin. Besides, Lane's persistent. He wouldn't have just accepted that you two were over. He would have had questions—questions I wasn't prepared to answer because you and your parents explicitly told me not to say a word. I didn't see any other way to handle it." Nicolino gently squeezed her shoulders. "Don't worry. I had a talk with Lane earlier and he knows the deal."

"The deal." Lucy sighed. While she welcomed Nicolino's help, she didn't want to be coddled, either. "Just what is this deal? I got the distinct impression that Lane still holds a grudge."

Nicolino slapped his thigh. "Dammit, I thought he and I had an understanding."

"Don't you dare pass this off on Lane," Ella hissed. "I told you to tell them both before Lucy arrived. You chose not to. Now look at the mess you've already made. I knew I should've told them both myself."

Lucy stepped between the two of them. "Would one of you please explain what's going on?"

Nicolino kicked at the dirt. "Lane thought the barn manager position was his."

"He what?" Lucy covered her mouth for fear of what might come out of it. No wonder he was angry. "When did he find out the job wasn't his?" she asked from behind her fingers.

"When I made the announcement this morning." Nicolino held up his hands. "And before you both rip into me, Lane did a fine enough job of that already. I was wrong. I admit it. I should've told him as soon as I offered you the—"

"Dio mio." Lucy looked heavenward. "You only hired me to get us here." Nicolino turned his back

to them. "I'm right, aren't I?" Lucy grabbed his arm and forced him to face her. "Lane told me he's my second-in-command. He earned the promotion, didn't he? I've wondered why you offered me the job, since I don't have any experience outside of the horses Antonio owned. I thought this was a sign from above, but it was you playing God."

"You're better off here than over there," Nicolino argued. "And you're wrong. You are qualified. You should be proud of your education."

"I am proud. Proud enough to know you hired me because I'm your cousin." Lucy wasn't sure what to do. It was her first day and her employees already had good reason to hate her. "You could have asked us to come, anyway. I would have found something else. You do realize you've pitted me against my ex-boyfriend, right? If I were smart, I should demand you give the job to Lane and work under him until I found something else."

"No, you won't," Nicolino retorted. "Lane is very good, but he doesn't have the education or the experience with the employees. I've been to your estate and I've attended your black-tie affairs. You've managed a large staff. You also have a presence and a way with people. Lane's rough around the edges, where you're much more refined. We need someone to stay on top of the latest equine advancements and work closely with our vets and clients. Lane doesn't have that polish."

"The staff I had hardly compares to the size of this ranch." Lucy rubbed her forehead in a vain bid to thwart the pounding in her skull. "Relax, I'm not going anywhere. I need this job too much to walk away from it."

The pressure had increased exponentially now that she knew she'd stolen a job from a man she once loved. A man against whom she had repeatedly measured her husband. Oh, she had loved Antonio, but she'd never been *in* love with him. The feeling had been mutual. He'd taken good care of her, but they'd never found the romance they'd both craved.

Lucy had been distraught when she'd discovered she was carrying Lane's baby. He'd been resolute about not having kids and had always made certain they used protection. When the experts said no birth control was 100 percent effective, they weren't kidding. Uncertain of what she should do next, Lucy had turned to her older sister for advice, who then immediately betrayed her confidence and told their parents. They had insisted she marry immediately. Lucy being unwed and pregnant with a Texas ranchhand's child would have tarnished the family's name in their small village—something her parents refused to allow.

Antonio—a longtime family friend and ten years her senior—had agreed to be her husband. The decision to marry Antonio and not tell Lane she was pregnant had been heart wrenching. She'd known Lane wasn't ready to take on the responsibility of a child, especially when he was beginning a new job in Wyoming—never mind how disgraced her parents would have been if the truth surrounding her baby's paternity had gotten out. Eighteen and scared, Lucy had felt the need to secure her baby's future and married Antonio in a civil ceremony a week later. Only Antonio and Lucy's family knew who her child's father really was.

"I'm going back to work." There was no point continuing the argument when she had no intention of quitting. They'd have to find a way to get along, despite the past. "I'll pick Carina up from your house later."

"You're welcome to join us for dinner. That is, if you can stand being around my husband after what he's done." Ella glowered at Nicolino.

Lucy laughed. She wanted to stay mad at her cousin, but she knew he'd kept Lane a secret only in order to protect her. Lane probably wouldn't have been very understanding and she couldn't blame him.

"I think we'll pass." Lucy was still digesting the rich Southern food from the previous night's dinner. "I have a lot to discuss with Carina before she starts school tomorrow. I'm still debating whether I should drive her or allow her to take the bus."

"Let me know either way," Ella said. "She won't be alone if she takes the bus. Lord knows she'll have enough cousins there with her."

Regardless of how Lucy felt about Nicolino's little deception, Ramblewood was the best place for Carina. She'd always been close to her cousins on Antonio's side, but after the divorce, they'd kept their distance. Lucy could adjust to almost anything; Carina was much more sensitive and didn't accept change well.

Even though her daughter appeared tough on the outside, her silence was louder than any scream.

Lucy climbed back into her car and pulled around to the ranch's parking lot. A knot formed in her stomach at the thought of facing Lane again. She mentally prepared herself as she trudged down the path to the stables. The mid-September air seemed heavier than it had a few minutes ago at the main house. The scrape of a shovel against the cement floor greeted her as the sweet scent of hay tickled her nose. Out of everything she'd lost in Italy, Lucy missed their horses the most. She made her way down the exposed-timber hallway as snorts sounded from behind the full-height mahogany stall doors.

The building branched off in four directions from the main hub where Nicolino had introduced her to everyone earlier. She flattened herself against the wall as a groom led two horses past. She knew where the main offices were, but after that she was clueless. She reached into her bag and withdrew a notebook. The first order of business was to sketch a map. *Helpless* was twice as profane as any four-letter curse word and she refused to ever feel that way again. She started with what she knew and drew a big *X* in the center of the page.

"Looking for buried treasure?" Lane said, peering over her shoulder.

Lucy's hand flew to her chest. "You startled me." She looked up at him. His straw Stetson partially shaded his soul-searching deep brown eyes as they met hers. Subtle lines had creased his features over the years. A day's worth of stubble shadowed his upper lip and jawline. While he appeared harder than she remembered, his expression had softened since earlier that day. And he was close. So close his breath kissed her cheek. "I—I feel like I need to leave a popcorn trail around here." She shifted, creating more of a distance between them. "I can't believe how much has changed."

"It's been a while." Lane sighed loudly and started down one of the corridors. "Come on, let's make a map."

"Uh…are you sure?" Lucy needed someone to show her around, but she had no doubt there were many other people who could handle the task. Anyone besides Lane would do. "I don't want to keep you from anything."

"You're keeping me from my promotion." Lane halted midstep and turned to face her. "I'm sorry. That was uncalled for. I'm still trying to accept losing the job I thought I had on top of my ex-girlfriend's sudden reappearance. You have to admit it's a potent combination." For a moment, Lucy thought he was about to take her hand in his. He didn't, and she wasn't sure why that made her a touch sad. It certainly would have been inappropriate if he had. "I'd love to say it's not personal," he continued, "but we both know a part of it is. I hate this, but there's more to it. And I'm not sure if it's me finally getting some closure or if it's because I'm happy to see you again."

Lucy steadied herself with a few deep breaths. *This can't be happening. I can't still have feelings for Lane.*

The guilt she carried after losing their baby four months into the pregnancy had never faded. Their son never took his first breath or said his first words. She never had the chance to hold him in her arms or even kiss him goodbye. She'd named him Lane, much to her family's dismay, but Antonio had understood and supported her decision. She'd lost both Lanes and her heart wasn't strong enough to let one back in without the other.

GIVING LUCY A tour was the absolute last thing Lane wanted to do, but he wasn't going to walk away from his job just yet. The physical closeness to Lucy was almost unbearable. The honey scent of her long mahogany hair was intoxicating and distracting at the same time. He wondered if her skin still felt as silky as it once had beneath his rough palms. Thoughts he shouldn't think churned in his mind. The woman had been back in his life for a few hours and already she'd gotten to him.

"Tell me about the ranch you worked on in Italy." Considering Nicolino had introduced Lucy using her maiden name, he wanted to ask about her husband, but he resolved to keep it professional. "What horses did you breed?"

"I—I didn't." Her voice was barely audible. "I went to school and managed the horses on our estate."

Lane froze at the entrance to the grain room. "Estate?" He hadn't expected that answer. "How many horses did you have?"

"Twenty." Lucy reached past him and opened the door, leaving him standing in the hallway.

Lane forced himself to follow her inside despite his shock at her response. "You do realize this is the state's largest paint and cutting horse ranch, right?"

Lucy cleared her throat. "Yes, Lane. I'm well aware of its size. Thank you for reminding me, though."

How could Nicolino hire someone with zero hands-on experience? If that wasn't a kick in the teeth. No—she wouldn't last. He'd give her a week before she realized how unprepared she was. He'd help Lucy, but no way would he train her. It took years of apprenticeship to learn the job and he wasn't about to mentor his boss. Lane doubted it would ever come to that. If Lucy didn't realize she was underqualified, then the Langtrys ultimately would. They prided themselves on the quality of Bridle Dance stock, and inexperience meant safety concerns. Lane might take issue with Nicolino, but allowing the company to suffer was not an option. Until he could prove Lucy unsuitable, he'd have to ensure she did nothing to harm the operation, the horses or herself. He didn't relish having to babysit his ex-girlfriend.

Lane continued to show Lucy around each wing of the Bridle Dance stables and introduced her to the majority of the people on the day staff. The state-of-the-art breeding lab fascinated Lucy the most and her knowledge of the process surprised him. There had been a breeding program in place when she'd last visited Ramblewood, but it had grown significantly since then. Maybe a nudge or two in that direction would tempt her to explore other options. He'd prefer her off the ranch entirely, but that wasn't his choice to make. Seeing her in any other position would be more tolerable than in the one he'd earned.

"Here's our home base." Lane opened the door to a small room located on the main stable floor near the entrance. One thing he hadn't factored in was that they'd be sharing an office. Not that they'd have the opportunity to spend much time in it together. The majority of their day would be spent either in the stables or outside. Being next to her inside the cramped space just about short-circuited his brain. He noticed beads of sweat forming above her lip and he wondered if she was nervous about being alone with him or if she was hot from the relentless September heat. He didn't dare ask.

Even though he hated that Lucy had the job he wanted, he couldn't blame her for getting an education. He was the same age, and she was a reminder that he should be further along in his career. He'd been on his own since his eighteenth birthday. Lucy had been a year older when she'd had Carina. He gave her credit for raising a child while going to college.

Lane sat at the desk across from hers. He cleared his throat. "It's rare that we'll have a chance to sit down like this during most days. Is there anything you want to ask that I haven't already covered? I'm all yours." He wanted to take back the words the moment he'd said them. Flirting with Lucy was not an option, not that he was attempting to flirt with her.

He would not ride down that trail again, especially now that he knew the extent of her betrayal.

Lucy flipped open her notebook and removed a sheet of paper printed on both sides, resembling a scan from a classroom workbook rather than something she'd typed. Couldn't she have come up with her own questions to ask? "How often does the farrier come in?"

"He never leaves. Well, we allow him to go home at night. We have an on-site farrier named Jorge—he works exclusively for Bridle Dance. He's responsible for all shoeing and hoof trimming."

"Who manages that schedule?" Lucy continued to take notes without bothering to look at him. He should have been relieved, but he found it almost dismissive. Okay, so their time together had ended a decade ago; it was still history—a lot of history. He wasn't a stranger, yet she was treating him like one.

It was a battle to concentrate on her questions and not ask any of his own. "You do." Lane stood and pulled a binder from the shelf. The movement caused her to glance up at him. When their gazes met, he instantly regretted wishing for eye contact moments ago. Unprepared for the disruption to his thought process, his mind struggled for words. "It's impossible..." Lane cleared his throat again. "It's impossible for you to check every horse on the ranch yourself. We have a schedule depending on the horse's age, what stage of training it's in, its activity level and so on. We handle the yearlings more frequently, so they'll get accustomed to the process. This allows us to see if they require any corrective shoeing. Jorge will email you a daily log sheet and you'll need to print, review and file it in here every day."

Lane felt as though he were talking at warp speed. After he'd explained employee schedules, payroll procedures and supply ordering and had answered every question she had asked, the afternoon was almost over. It was too much time together—too much closeness. He was wrong before. The past needed to stay in the past. Too many of the times they'd shared together thrashed wildly in his brain like a bull trying to buck its rider. Lane stood and reached for the doorknob, wondering why he'd ever closed the door in the first place. "There's also a checklist we run through at the end of the day and give to Brad—the night manager—when he comes in, which should be shortly. He'll repeat the same process in the morning with you. We'll cover that tomorrow."

Lucy's fingers lightly brushed against his arm as she tried to stop him before he opened the door. The singe of heat he felt from the brief contact lasted only a second before she apologetically stepped back. "I know I told you earlier that this wasn't the place to discuss what happened, but I need you to know that I'm sorry for the way things ended. I didn't know you waited for me in Wyoming. I thought Nicolino had told you and that's my fault. You deserved a personal explanation from me. I also found out you wanted this job. If I had known, I never would have accepted the position. But that doesn't mean I'm going to walk away from it, either."

"This morning was a complete surprise." Lane folded his arms. "Nicolino claims you're more qualified than me. While that remains to be seen, I'll admit that I'm surprised at the career path you chose, considering the way you used to party when we were kids. I always knew you were smart. I just never knew you had the commitment to stay with something." Lane cringed at his own words. "That didn't come out exactly how I meant it. Let's just say…you were much more free-spirited back then. Your dedication and commitment to your education is commendable, along with raising a beautiful daughter. It couldn't have been easy."

"Thank you. It wasn't exactly part of my grand plan, but I can't imagine life without Carina." Lucy dropped her gaze, shifting from one foot to the other. "The circumstances surrounding my marriage to Antonio were far from ideal. The love we shared for our daughter kept us together, especially after we almost lost her. Carina was born three months premature. Her chances for survival were almost nonexistent. I can't even begin to tell you what that was like. I wouldn't wish that pain on my worst enemy."

"I had no idea you even had a child until yesterday." A part of him wasn't sure he was ready to hear about the child she'd had with some other man; another part wanted to know everything about her life since he'd last seen her. "What happened?"

Lucy's eyes shone with wetness. "The majority of my pregnancy was spent bedridden. When I went into labor, they didn't think either one of us would

survive. I refused to give up on her. Watching your
child lie there helpless inside an incubator, connected
to tubes and wires while a machine breathes for her,
is beyond words. I knew every beep, every hum from
the equipment in the room. Carina's a fighter." She
met his eyes once again. "I'm sorry if the news of my
marriage hurt you. It wasn't all wine and roses, but it
wasn't terrible, either. Antonio loved Carina. He…"

Lane straightened his spine, still trying to wrap
his head around what she had told him and what she
had purposely left out. "He what? What happened
to Antonio?"

Lucy sighed. "Antonio died of a brain aneurysm
four months ago."

Lane had wondered if Carina's father was still involved in her life. Death had been the furthest possibility from his mind. He understood the anguish her
daughter probably felt, having lost his own father as
a child. "That must've been incredibly difficult for
you both."

"We'd been divorced for almost a year when it
happened, but we had remained very close. Antonio was my best friend. But there were things I
didn't know. Like how much debt he had. We lived
well—too well. After he died, I discovered some
of his business affairs were not—how do I say it in
English?—legitimate. All of his assets were seized
and we were left with nothing. We didn't even have
my family's support after he died. If you thought they
were strict when I was growing up, that was nothing compared to what happened after Antonio and

I divorced. They disowned us. Try explaining that to a kid." Lucy's nervous laughter reminded him of the summer they'd met, when she'd opened up about her parents' harsh criticism. He wanted to wrap her in his arms and comfort her as he'd once done. "My divorce and his business improprieties disgraced the Travisonno family name. No one else will communicate with us except Nicolino and Ella. And that's why we're here. I never meant to create problems for you."

Lucy's declaration made him feel guilty for being angry at her at first. He didn't want to be mad and he definitely didn't want to hate her. He wished they could go back and do things over, but that was wishful thinking and Lane didn't have a wishful bone in his body.

"At least I'm not the only one Nicolino kept in the dark." Lane attempted a laugh but his heart wasn't in it after everything Lucy had told him. "I'm willing to put the past behind us, not that it's going to be easy. I'll try my best, though. What do you say we start over?" Lane extended his hand as a peace offering.

Lucy nodded. Her face brightened again, sending a twinge of anticipation through his chest. The instant they touched, their fingers entwined, and not in your typical handshake. *So much for starting over.* The feel of her skin against his was better than in his memories. The heat from her palm seared into his. He knew she felt it, too, when she tightened her grip. He wanted to pull her into his arms, to kiss her the way he used to, but he couldn't. Lane closed his eyes. He couldn't do this with her—not now, not ever again.

"I'm sorry." Releasing her, he flung open the door and strode into the safety of the corridor. "There's always someone here, 24/7, and as barn manager, you are on call, too. Which reminds me, I need your phone number."

"I don't have one yet." She spoke so quietly he barely heard her.

"We can rectify that right now. Follow me and we'll get you set up with a company phone. Then that will be it for the day."

Lane led the way up the stairs to the administrative offices, praying the torrent of emotions running through him wouldn't get the best of him. He needed to remain professional and carefully plan his next move. He was torn between proving his worth to Nicolino and looking for another position. Lucy's earlier questions and wide-eyed gaze at some of his answers reconfirmed she was unqualified for the practical aspects of the job.

Lucy clearly needed the money more than he did, but Lane was doubtful she'd be able to handle the workload. Book smarts weren't everything. If he left and she failed, the position he'd worked so hard for would go to someone else. If he stayed around, then he'd have a chance at righting a wrong. But his attraction to Lucy was already proving too great for him to maintain a working relationship without losing his heart in the process. He wasn't ready to walk away from either one…at least not yet.

Chapter Three

"Are you sure you don't want me to drive you?" Lucy asked.

Carina rolled her eyes. "Mamma, the other kids are already going to talk about me. Let me walk into school on my own. I'm a big girl. I'll handle it."

That had become Carina's motto lately. A soon-to-be nine-year-old shouldn't have to handle things. She should be outside playing and spending time with friends. Not starting over in a new country because her parents had failed to provide for her on their own. At least it was Friday and they'd both have the weekend to allow the past few days to sink in.

"Okay I'll drop you off at Ella and Nicolino's and you can walk to the bus with your cousins." Lucy didn't know which of them was more nervous about Carina's first day of school. "I'm not letting you walk from here. The ranch is too big and you don't know your way around."

Carina shrugged and waited for her by the front door. Why was she finding it so difficult to send her child off to school? She should have been excited for all the new adventures she was about to have. Since the day Carina was born, Lucy had hated relinquishing her daughter's care to somebody else. She knew all the facts and read all the books about change being necessary for a child's growth and development. It didn't make things any easier, though. *Once you see your child fight to live, you never want to let them go.*

"Try to have fun today and call if you need me. I put my new number in your backpack and I'll pick you up a cell phone by the end of the day. *Ti amo, mia gattina.*"

"I love you, too, Mamma," she replied, surprisingly in English.

Lucy dropped Carina off with her cousins and continued down the ranch road to work. It felt good to have a job and be able to earn her own money. Antonio had always given her a generous allowance, but she'd never felt as if anything had truly been hers.

Lucy wondered how long it would take before she stopped thinking about Antonio every five minutes. She laughed inwardly. She remembered asking herself the same question about Lane years ago. The problem was he had never been far from her mind. She didn't think a day had gone by that she hadn't thought of him and wondered what he was doing. She'd envisioned him married and still living in Wyoming. Clearly she'd been wrong about Wyoming, but what about the married part? She'd been so wrapped up in her own world that she hadn't thought to ask him about his family or his life over the past ten years.

"I can do this. I need to do this." The mantra had

given her strength on the darkest of days, reminding Lucy that she had the power to rebuild their lives. She braced for another day with Lane as she stepped out of the car. It had pained her to lie to him yesterday. But he didn't need to know about her first pregnancy. Nothing would change the fact that she'd lost their baby. Partying in Texas combined with the inordinate amount of stress she'd been under from her family and the whirlwind marriage to Antonio had proved too much for their baby.

She'd been devastated by her miscarriage. After she'd heard her baby's heartbeat for the first time, she couldn't imagine loving anyone more. She had wanted that back. Antonio had remained by her side and cared for her through the entire ordeal, promising her another child when she was ready. Six months later, she was pregnant again. Carina was the greatest gift Antonio had ever given her.

Lucy took a deep breath and entered the stables. After meeting briefly with the night barn manager, she attempted to track down her employees. It was a daunting task since she didn't know where anyone was. She hadn't seen Lane or Nicolino and wasn't sure where she was supposed to begin the day.

Waiting inside her office, Lucy tried to familiarize herself with the numerous charts, log sheets and binders that filled every inch of space in the room. Morning meetings would be the first thing she implemented into their daily routine. It baffled her how they'd ever survived without them. It was basic employee management.

If Lucy had checked her phone once, she'd checked it a hundred times by ten o'clock. No call from her daughter was a good sign. She knew none of the changes over the past year, especially the move, had been easy for Carina. For her own sanity, Lucy phoned the school. She began to relax when they reassured her that Carina was fine and in class. As she hung up, she noticed Lane standing in the doorway of their office, concern etched upon his face.

"Is everything all right?"

"Yes." Lucy smiled so big she thought her lips might split. "My daughter is in class and she's doing wonderfully. Thank you for asking. Do you have any children?" Lucy wanted to ask him if he'd ever married but feared it would be too forward. She held her breath waiting for him to answer, praying he'd say no. If he'd never had kids, then her reasons for keeping her secret all these years might prove valid— perhaps he'd never been ready.

Lane's eyes grew large at the question. "Ah…no." He laughed. "No kids, no wife. Just a few surly bunkmates. I live on the ranch, too. Bunkhouse A."

The elation that grew at Lane's response confused her. She wouldn't let herself care one way or the other about that little fact. Lane was her employee. "How is your mom?"

"Still here, God bless her." Lane removed his hat. "She's a little older, but aren't we all?"

Why did he do that? The sight of his thick dark hair made her fingers itch with the desire to run through it. "Glad to hear it." Lucy refocused on her notebook.

"Listen, I'd like to organize a daily meeting with everyone beginning tomorrow. Something brief so we can run down what's planned for the day. The earlier, the better."

"Um…okay. That might cut into some people's schedules, though. Everyone arrives at different times. Plus, the schedules rotate weekly." Lane pulled a binder from the bookcase and opened it on the desk. Lucy fought to ignore the way his arm brushed hers as he pointed to the first page. "We briefly touched on this yesterday. The current one is always on top. It's just a printout from our stable-management software. Curly found using a printout faster than logging on to the computer every time he needed to see who was working where." Lane rapidly turned the pages, creating a slight vibration against her skin. "If you look through the previous months, you'll notice a pattern in the rotation."

Lucy tried to make sense of the pages Lane flipped through, but his closeness made it difficult to concentrate. She flattened her palms on top of the binder, causing him to retreat. *Thank you.* "I'm capable of reading a schedule. How am I supposed to know what's going on around here without a daily meeting?"

Lane propped an elbow on the filing cabinet and rubbed the side of his jaw. "Lucy, this is a quarter-of-a-million-acre ranch. We have employees coming in at daybreak who have very specific feeding times to adhere to. You can't ask them to stop what they're doing to attend a meeting. It'll set off a chain reaction that will affect the meds, turnout and muck schedules. This is a huge operation and we've painstakingly planned it to maintain balance. I understand your reasoning, but not everyone works in or near the stables. You have employees out in the pastures, too. Everyone has a two-way radio." Lane crossed the tiny office in three strides. He unplugged one of the radios and handed it to her. "You can get in touch with the people who aren't in your immediate vicinity on here. Try not to tie up the frequency band with long conversations, though. Call them on the phone or take a utility vehicle out to wherever they are instead. If you want to see who's clocked in or out, you can pull it up on the computer."

Lucy ground her teeth together. She pulled her hair back at her nape and loosely knotted it while she attempted to formulate a response. This was exactly what she'd meant when she'd told Nicolino she didn't have the practical experience for the job. Someone who'd apprenticed for years under a barn manager would know these things.

A sting of heat rose to her cheeks. "I will take your suggestions under advisement. Thank you." She wished he'd leave so she could review the schedules without him watching her every move.

Lane lowered himself onto the chair next to her and set his hat upside down on the corner of the desk. "I'm going to offer you a little unsolicited advice. Instead of focusing on what you feel needs to change, concentrate on what you don't know."

"Such as?" Lucy wasn't sure she wanted to hear

the answer, but she was certain being alone with him in the small room was making it increasingly difficult to breathe.

"When was the last time you rode with a Western saddle? Better yet, when was the last time you saddled a Western horse?"

Lucy tapped a pen against her notebook. "The last time I was here."

"Then that's where you need to begin. There will be days when you'll need to saddle a horse and get out there with the rest of us. I'll pair you up with one of the grooms and they'll walk you through the entire process of saddling a cutting horse and get you accustomed to riding Western again. You should shadow some of the trainers and ride a few of the cutting horses. You need to understand what we do and how we do it in order to run this facility."

These were all things she'd thought about last night. She just hadn't wanted to hear them from the man she knew still wanted her job. "Thanks, but these things are already on my list."

"Okay, then." Lane rose, grabbed his hat and strode to the office door. "I'll leave you to it, boss."

Boss? Great—attitude. She hadn't expected anything less, and if she were honest with herself, he gave as good as she did.

After fumbling her way through the majority of the day, Lucy ran into town to pick up a phone for Carina. She couldn't wait to get home to hear how her day had gone.

Shortly after Lucy arrived at the cottage, Ella

stopped by to drop off Carina. When Lucy opened the front door, Carina made a beeline inside without a word. Lucy thanked Ella for bringing her daughter home, then said goodbye and closed the door, trailing after Carina. She yelped, practically tripping over a backpack on the floor. Usually her daughter wasn't so careless. Seeing Carina's bedroom door closed, she knocked—no answer. She tried the knob—locked. Typical Carina. Lock the door, pop in the earbuds and crank up the iPod. It used to infuriate Antonio. Luckily, their cottage was on one level. Lucy walked around the side of the house and found Carina's bedroom window open. She climbed inside, scaring her daughter half to death.

"That'll teach you." Lucy grinned and gently tugged on Carina's earbuds.

"What do you want?" Carina snarled in Italian.

What happened to the sweet little girl with the cheery disposition I raised? "How was school?"

"I hate it." Carina pouted.

"Did you give it a chance?" Lucy sat on the edge of the twin-size bed. Her daughter had had a king-size one in their villa.

"Yes," Carina huffed. "They talk fast and I don't know what my homework is."

"Did you ask your teacher to write it down for you?"

"No." She shook her head. "I didn't want to look stupid."

"I'll call the school on Monday and ask the teacher to write out your assignments." Lucy stopped Carina from putting her earbuds back in. "You can't give up. It's not easy for me, either."

"Fine."

Lucy stood, knowing she was about to be tuned out once again. "What would you like for dinner?"

"Nothing."

One-word answers. *Lovely.* "Okay, I'll leave you alone, but keep the door unlocked or I'll take it off the hinges. Oh, before I forget." Lucy fished the new cell phone from her pocket and handed it to Carina. "For you."

"Great, now I have a phone and no one to call."

Lucy threw her hands in the air and left the room. Skipping dinner, she sank into one of the white rocking chairs on the front porch. A refreshing breeze ruffled the collar of her Bridle Dance polo shirt. A lush green palette of the Texas Hill Country danced before her as the sun began to cast evening shadows against the house. The view was still gorgeous. She had seen her first American sunset with Lane. They'd been barely fourteen that first summer. He had placed his hat on her head, kissed her cheek and called her his Italian cowgirl. What she wouldn't give to relive that moment again. There used to be so much hope in the unknown, before life became scary and real. She missed those days… More important, she missed those days with Lane.

LANE POPPED THE top off a longneck and sat on the wooden front steps of the bunkhouse. The setting sun reminded him of Lucy. It always had.

"Do you want a burger?" Rusty asked from behind the grill.

He eased his body up, grabbed a plate and heaped a spoonful of the older man's famous mac and cheese onto it. He fixed his burger and joined the rest of his bunkmates at the picnic table.

"How's the boss lady working out?" one of them asked. "Didn't you used to date her? It's gotta suck working for your ex-girlfriend."

Lane groaned, opting to take a bite of his burger instead of answering.

"Hey, kid," Rusty began. "Far be it from me to stick my nose in your business, but are you sure that kid ain't yours?"

Lane shot him a death glare. "You're right. It's none of your business, but I'll set the record straight before that rumor spreads and Carina or one of her cousins catches wind of it. Lucy and I have already had that conversation. She isn't mine. She's not even the right age."

While it hurt to know Lucy had gone home to Italy and had another man's child while he'd been planning a future with her, a part of him had been equally relieved Carina wasn't his daughter. He hadn't been ready for kids back then. He wasn't sure if he was ready now, but he'd given the idea more thought lately. Despite Nicolino's never giving him enough credit, he envied the man's relationship with Ella. Their lives were crazy and loud with five kids, but even as disorganized and frazzled as they sometimes were, they were happy.

"I think you should ask her out," Rusty said between bites. "You're far from strangers, and Lord knows, you've been pining over her ever since she left."

"Since when did you become a matchmaker?" a ranch hand asked.

"I've done more livin' than all of you combined. That entitles me to give advice."

Lane laughed. "You noticed he said advice, not *good* advice."

"Where's the kid's father?"

"He died four months ago, and the kid's name is Carina." Lucy had bombarded him with questions all day. He didn't want to answer more, especially any that pertained to her. "Do me a favor and let it drop."

They finished their meal talking about trucks and the new female bull-riding instructor at the rodeo school adjacent to the stables. It was nice seeing other men make fools of themselves over women so it wasn't just him.

"The way I see it, you and Lucy are doing the Texas two-step." A collective round of groans accompanied an onslaught of wadded-up napkins aimed at Rusty.

"You might as well hear him out and then maybe he'll shut up," a ranch hand said.

Lane set his beer on the table and faced Rusty. "Okay, this is your one shot. Lay it on me."

"All I'm sayin' is, you best be damn sure you don't want a second chance with her, because she's an attractive woman and this place is filled with cowboys who'd ride through fire for a chance to whirl her around the dance floor."

He hadn't thought of that. He looked around the table at his bunkmates. "I swear, if any of you ask her out, I'll—"

"Relax." Rusty smacked Lane on the shoulder. "She couldn't handle a man like me."

Everyone laughed. Lane didn't think he had to worry about a 75-year-old ranch hand going after Lucy. Rusty had a point, though. Lane had no claim to Lucy and she was free to date whomever she wanted. So why did the thought of it gnaw at the pit of his stomach?

Lane checked his pockets for his keys and wallet and excused himself from the table. "I'll catch up with you guys later."

He started his truck with no real direction in mind but somehow found himself pulling in front of Lucy's cottage fifteen minutes later. He hadn't noticed her watching him from the porch while he gathered up his nerve to talk to her. Wonderful. Now he had some explaining to do.

He climbed out of his truck and silently joined her on the front porch, watching the sun make its final descent beyond the horizon.

"I was just sitting here thinking about you." Her admission offered him a little more confidence.

"What a coincidence," Lane said. "I'll tell you mine if you tell me yours."

Lucy faced him, her head still resting against the

rocking chair. "I was remembering the first sunset I saw in this country."

"That was with me, wasn't it?"

Lucy nodded, a slow, easy smile forming as she closed her eyes. "My first night in Texas. I was in Ramblewood Park eating ice cream and you sat beside me on the bleachers."

"I can still remember how nervous I was to talk to you." He watched her smile broaden as her eyes opened lazily. He wanted to pull her into his arms and kiss her—slowly, as though they had all the time in the world to experience each other all over again.

"You and I had a good thing once." She turned back to the horizon. As soon as she'd broken eye contact, he ached for it again.

It was every man's fantasy to hear his first love admit she still thought of him, but Lane wasn't prepared for the pain of actually hearing the words. "We were kids. Neither one of us knew what we were doing or where we were going. I won't deny what I felt for you was real, because it was, but as much as I'd love to go back in time, we're not those people anymore."

"I'd like to think we're better," she said.

"I'll give you that." He reached for her hand and gave it a gentle squeeze. The instant he touched her, Lane knew he shouldn't have come. He needed to get in his truck and leave her and the past alone before his heart paid the price again.

"And stronger," Lucy said as she withdrew from him, resting her hands on her lap.

"Don't forget wiser. Although that might be debatable on my part right about now." Lane laughed at the irony of his own words. He attempted to will himself off the porch and back to the bunkhouse without success. This was a mistake.

"What am I doing wrong?" Lucy asked while gazing out into the fields before them.

Lane wondered if it was a rhetorical question or if he should answer. "In regards to what?"

"Everything. My daughter misses her father and hates me because I moved us to America. My new job's a bit overwhelming and I have feelings for you that I've never been able to get rid of."

Lane blew out a breath. "I see you haven't lost your brutal honesty. Do you really want me to answer your question?"

"Go for it." Lucy's eyes connected with his and for a moment, he envisioned kissing her.

Lane turned his rocking chair toward her. "For starters, I think all kids hate their parents." He reached over and tucked a strand of hair behind her ear, allowing its silkiness to slide through his fingers before retreating. "You could move her to the other side of the world or make the wrong thing for breakfast and probably get the same reaction. We did it. Our parents did it. It's human nature. Carina's had a lot more to deal with than most kids her age. Please don't get mad at me for asking, but have you considered a child psychologist to give her someone neutral to talk to?"

"I tried that in Italy but all she did was sit in the

chair and stare at the wall. She refused to talk. When Carina shuts you out, you're shut out. I haven't found a way to get through to her yet. I hear her talk to the animals all the time, but I'm sure that's because she can say what she wants to them and they won't repeat it."

"Talking to animals sounds like normal childhood behavior to me. Lord knows I did it." Lane welcomed her willingness to confide in him about Carina, but he couldn't help wondering why she wasn't talking to Ella instead of him. "Learning your new job will take some time. You're not going to want to hear it, but this is exactly why people apprentice for this position."

Lucy sighed and shook her head.

"Hey, you asked." He might want Lucy to give up her job, but not if it meant her giving up on herself. "Look at how long I've been doing this—and according to your cousin, I'm still not ready. It's not going to be easy. I'm not saying you can't do it—I'm just saying you need to focus on one particular task at a time. I don't know what they taught you in school, but, honey, this job takes years to learn and decades to master. You can't squeeze it into a couple of training sessions."

"I should be angry at that statement," Lucy said.

"But you're not?"

"No. I hope you can be patient with me while I muddle through it." She rested her hand on his. "I appreciate your help so far, even though I know how disappointed you are." The warmth of her touch sent a lone shiver down his spine. "Now it's your turn. What were you thinking about me before you showed up here? You sat in your truck awhile before you even got out."

"I was hoping you hadn't noticed." Lane attempted to laugh. He wasn't used to being nervous around women, let alone the woman who used to make him feel more comfortable than anyone else had. "I was thinking about us and what could have been."

Lucy quickly rose and moved to the far corner of the porch. A minute of silence passed between them. "What we had is gone," she said without facing him. "You and I have grown in opposite directions. You're still doing what you love—what you know. I've faced a lot of uncertainty. As difficult as it's been at times, I can't imagine life without my daughter, and that's something you never wanted."

"Be fair. That was a long time ago. The last time you and I discussed kids, we were teenagers. Many of my friends have kids now, and yes, I've thought about it. I've thought about it a lot. If the situation presented itself, I would definitely consider it." Lane stopped before he said more than he intended to. He crossed the porch to join her—close enough to sense her body tense but apparently not close enough to hear her breathe, making him wonder if she held her breath in anticipation of what he'd do next. "When I'm with you, I have difficulty breathing the same air you breathe. I can honestly say I've never gotten over you. And here you are, back in my life. You're my boss and you're the last person I need to get involved with, but I don't know how to be around you and not want you."

"We can't," Lucy whispered as she turned to face him.

Lane barely heard her words before their lips met. Her body instantly softened beneath his touch. Tugging her closer, he wrapped his arms tightly around her waist. Her lips parted slightly as he probed the recesses of her mouth with his tongue. She tasted exactly as he remembered. Sweet and warm, like farm-fresh honey. They broke their kiss and stared into each other's eyes.

"My sweet Italian cowgirl, I've missed you." Lane released her and took a step backward. His chest ached. He was torn between wanting to pull her closer and walking away forever. "You're right. We can't. I refuse to put myself through that pain again. You married another man and got pregnant while I waited for you. How do I forgive that?"

"Then why did you come here?" Lucy demanded. "Why did you kiss me?"

Lane hadn't meant to hurt or confuse her. "I came because I hoped you had a reason that justified what you did. Something—anything—that would move us past it and maybe even allow us to start over." In his heart, he knew her reasons wouldn't change his mind. It was too late for them. "You haven't told me why and now I honestly don't want to know."

"Don't you think I know how hard it is to live with all the what-ifs? Or how hard it is to smile when all you keep thinking about is what you've lost and what will never be?" Lucy glanced at the front door and lowered her voice. "I may not have had a perfect marriage, but I don't regret marrying Antonio for one second."

"Wow!" Her words were a sucker punch to the gut. "I was looking for answers. Didn't expect that one, though."

"I wouldn't have my daughter if it hadn't been for him." Lucy's face reddened. "You can't begin to imagine the bond that forms when you create a child with someone."

"You're right. I can't," Lane said. "You never gave us that chance. I loved you. And if we're completely honest, I've loved only you. I would have done anything for you and if you had really wanted a family once we had established ourselves in Wyoming, I would have given it to you. You stole that opportunity from me. Now you've stolen my job."

"You need to accept the past and realize I'm not leaving here, regardless of how unqualified you think I am. I will do whatever it takes to provide for my daughter and myself. We're not looking for handouts, even though that's exactly what you think Nicolino gave us. My cousin believes in me, and more important, I believe in me. While I'm busy proving you wrong, you need to keep your distance. We work together and that's it. Don't kiss me again."

"That's a promise I'll take to the grave." Lane stormed down the porch stairs. He heard the front door slam shut before he reached his truck. Score one for Lucy. She managed to get the best of him tonight, but that was the only point she'd win. She'd already taken too much from him; he refused to allow her to take his pride, too.

Chapter Four

"He kissed me. He's not allowed to kiss me," Lucy whispered across the kitchen table the following morning. She poured Ella a cup of coffee and set the pot between them. "I'm his boss. Besides, our past is…is just that—it's in the past. And stop laughing at me." She swatted Ella.

Ella ducked to the side, still giggling. "The lady doth protest too much."

"What's that supposed to mean?" Lucy prayed Carina hadn't overheard them from her bedroom. It was bad enough the feel of Lane's kiss still lingered on her lips… She didn't need her daughter asking questions, too.

"If you don't want a relationship with Lane, you won't have one. It's that simple." Ella heaped a spoonful of sugar into her cup and gave it a quick stir. "The way you're so animated about a kiss that happened twelve hours ago makes me think you're more interested in him than you're willing to admit."

"Are you kidding? I can't stand that man." It wasn't exactly a lie. It wasn't exactly the truth, either. Sometime in the middle of the night, she'd confessed—to herself—that she still found Lane incredibly attractive. It hadn't helped that he'd admitted she was the only woman he'd ever loved. Regardless of his declaration, a relationship was out of the question. Losing their son had been agonizing enough. Dating would be impossible with a secret of that magnitude between them. No—he could never know she'd married another man while carrying his child.

"You still haven't forgiven yourself, have you?" Ella patted her arm.

"Forgiven yourself for what?" Carina questioned from the doorway.

Lucy quickly stood, knocking her coffee cup onto the floor, shattering it. "Watch out." Lucy shooed Carina out of the way. "I don't want you to cut your feet."

"I'll get it." Ella grabbed a roll of paper towels from the counter to wipe up the mess. "Your mom and I were talking about her job. The first few days in a new place are always difficult—for everyone, including grown-ups."

"I need to get out of these clothes. Carina, will you please put your shoes on?" Lucy hurried to her bedroom and closed the door. A sob broke free. She slid down the wall, clutching her knees to her chest. She'd expected to relive some memories when she'd decided to move to Ramblewood, but Lane hadn't been part of the equation. Seeing him had opened old wounds, leaving her raw and vulnerable.

She rose from the floor and changed out of her coffee-stained clothes. After splashing cold water on her face, she stared at her reflection in the mirror. She was a mother first and she had to do whatever it took to provide for her daughter. Okay, so some renewed feelings for Lane had developed. They were nostalgic, not romantic. *They can't be romantic.* She wouldn't allow it.

Lucy made her way back to the kitchen, relieved her daughter wasn't there.

"She's outside on the front porch," Ella said. "Are you okay? You didn't get burnt, did you?"

Lucy shook her head. "I can trust that you won't discuss any part of my past with Lane at home or anywhere else, right? I'm afraid one of the kids might accidentally overhear a conversation and tell Carina. I shouldn't have even mentioned it with Carina in the house. You and Nicolino are the only ones who—"

Ella pulled her into a quick hug. "Shh. Say no more. You have my word."

"Thank you." Lucy stepped away. "I'm going to head down to the stables shortly. I need to refamiliarize myself with Western riding and I'm hoping Carina will join me, although that'll probably be one more thing that she'll accuse me of changing."

"But she loves to ride."

"She loves dressage and competing—at least, she did. Without Antonio's guidance, I'm afraid she won't ride again. When the horses were seized, Carina lost the last connection she had with her father." It was one more way her daughter felt Lucy had let her down. "There's a box full of ribbons and trophies in her room that she refuses to acknowledge. When

I have some extra cash, I'm hoping she'll be open to lessons again. I have no idea how I'm ever going to pay for a horse, though. And she'll definitely need new boots. The ones she insists on wearing are too tight, but she refuses to give them up because they were a gift from Antonio."

Carina shouldn't have had to give up anything. Kids shouldn't have to make sacrifices because their parents screwed up. Lucy hated that she had depended on Antonio for their sole support. She'd earned her degree and should've put it to use long before his death.

"Lucy, if you need money, we'll loan it to you—interest-free. Don't worry about that."

"Thank you, but that's how we got in this situation—by relying on others. I've got this."

And she did. At least, she would once she put Lane out of her mind.

Normally, Lane loved having the weekend to himself. Today he hated it. He had nothing to keep his mind off last night—and that kiss. Every memory he'd succeeded in shoving to the far recesses of his mind had returned thanks to his stupidity. He remembered their long talks and dreams for the future. The first time they'd made love—they'd been each other's firsts. The last kiss they'd shared. And the endless waiting to hear from Lucy, only to discover she'd found someone else. No—those memories needed to stay buried.

He'd already done his share of cleaning the bunkhouse and had paced the front porch twenty times before Rusty threw the newspaper at him.

"It didn't take long for you to get all torn up over Lucy again," the older man said. "The way I see it, you have two choices. Give her another chance or let it go for good. Either way, it won't be an easy decision. That's the trouble with cowgirls—they get under your skin like a bad tattoo. Even when you think you're well rid of them, they still leave a trace behind."

"Well, that was profound." Lane laughed. He had to admit there was some truth to Rusty's analogy, although he wouldn't exactly compare Lucy to a bad tattoo and she hadn't been a cowgirl for quite some time. "I think I might ride out and do some camping this weekend. I'm heading to the stables. You're welcome to join me, if you don't have anything else planned."

"And disappoint the ladies in town tonight?" Rusty feigned offense at Lane's suggestion. "You need some time alone to figure out what you want."

That was the problem. He knew what he wanted, and she was off-limits.

The Bridle Dance Ranch offered free horse boarding to resident employees. Not that paying any fee would've deterred him from keeping his beloved Frankie nearby. Besides his father's old turquoise 1967 Ford F100 pickup and the bare necessities, Frankie was all he owned—or rather, Frankie owned him. Lane had watched Frankie's birth and had been responsible for much of his training. When the Langtrys put him up for sale, Lane couldn't say goodbye, so he'd purchased him. A few days away with his trusty steed was exactly what he needed.

Minutes later, he heard Lucy shouting as he reached the stable entrance. Quickening his steps, he almost collided with Carina as she barreled down the walk.

He steadied her, double-checking she wasn't hurt. "I'm so sorry. Are you okay?"

Carina shrugged him off and faced her mother. "It's your fault."

Lane stepped out of her way as the pint-size version of Lucy stormed past him.

"Carina! Come back here." Lucy started to run after her daughter.

"Let her go." Lane reached out to stop her. He didn't need to know what was going on to understand Carina and Lucy needed a breather from each other. "She's just going toward the rodeo school. There are a lot of kids her age there this time of day."

Lucy glared at his hand wrapped around her upper arm and pulled away. He remembered when touching her didn't result in her wishing him dead. He released her, noticing the deep lines of frustration etched on her forehead.

"I don't need your help," she muttered.

"Actually, you do." Lane lowered his voice, guiding her away from the busy stable entrance and onto the grass, where they had a better view of the rodeo school. "Do you mind telling me what's going on?"

Lucy pulled her hair back into a ponytail, wrapping it with a band from her wrist. Her formfitting cream-colored riding breeches had definitely attracted the attention of every red-blooded man in the vicinity. Paired with her English riding boots, she definitely hadn't dressed for dusty cutting-horse riding.

"She misses our horses and her father. I thought while I brushed up on my Western skills that she might want to come along and try it, too. Once again, I was wrong. You should have heard her accusing me of trying to erase her father from our lives."

"Maybe you're trying too hard," Lane said.

"What would you know about it?" Lucy snapped. "You don't have kids."

It was easy to see where Carina got her attitude. "I was a little older than her when I lost my father. Granted, I didn't move to a new country, but it was hard enough. I rebelled against everything my mother asked me to do." He saw in her face that Lucy was bracing herself for a lecture, which Lane had no intention of giving. "I'm just saying, it may be better to allow her to make some of the decisions instead of you making all of them."

"I have been—at least, I'm trying to. I let her go shopping for school clothes without me."

"Speaking of which—" Lane appreciatively skimmed the length of her body "—you may want to tweak your own wardrobe a bit. You're attracting quite a bit of attention." *A little too much.*

"Give me a break." Lucy nervously looked around. "I spent the spare cash I had on my daughter. These are perfectly acceptable riding clothes. I realize I stand out, but there's nothing I can do about it."

"I'm sorry." Lane officially felt like a first-class jerk. "I wasn't thinking." They both watched Carina standing on the bottom rail of the rodeo school's fence. The small child's attention was transfixed on the barrel racers rounding the corral. "I get this is difficult for both of you. I'm not busy today, so why don't you go on to your lessons and I'll check on your daughter? Maybe you two just need a little space."

"Oh, I need space, but not from my daughter," Lucy ground out.

"After yesterday's incident, I really don't want to be around you, either." Lane had had enough tension for one day. "I'm sorry I kissed you. I assure you the mistake won't be repeated." The woman infuriated him. So he'd kissed her. Big deal. All right—so it had been a big deal. He'd wanted that kiss and it had been everything he'd remembered and more. But he had the right to be mad, not her. She'd left him, not the other way around.

"Shh." Lucy hushed him. "I don't need everybody knowing our business."

"Then don't stand in the stable entrance yelling after your daughter and people won't know your business," Lane scoffed. "I'm sure I don't need to remind you that everyone knows who you are, and you have an image to uphold. I won't tell Carina anything about you and me. Why don't you let me take her for the day? I'll show her around the rodeo school and the hippotherapy center and then I'll bring her back this afternoon. Maybe that'll be enough time for the two of you to cool down. That is, if you trust me."

Lucy eyed him reluctantly. "I've never had any reason not to trust you." Her words hung in the air as though she'd intended to say more but hadn't. She stepped out of the shadows into the morning sunlight, checking to ensure nobody was within earshot. "Maybe you're right. But promise me you—"

"Relax." Lane resisted the urge to tug her into his arms to comfort her, knowing it would cause World War III. "I already told you. I won't say a word, but enough people on this ranch know you and I dated at one point, so you might want to have that discussion with your daughter before someone else does."

Lane touched the brim of his hat in dismissal and crossed the parking lot to Carina. He stood beside her at the fence, silently watching the teenage girls weave their horses around the dirt course.

"My mom doesn't like you, does she?" Carina asked after a solid five minutes.

Lane inwardly laughed. "Where did that come from?"

"I heard her talking to Ella about you this morning." Carina's focus remained on the riders. "She sounded mad. Did you know her when she used to visit here?"

Lane looked over his shoulder, hoping Lucy would come rescue him. He feared answering her question would provoke more questions, but he didn't want to lie, either. "I did."

"Were you friends?"

Lane suppressed a groan. "We were." *Please, kid, don't ask me anything else about your mother.*

"What is that called?" Carina pointed to the horses.

Lane silently thanked the good Lord above for the subject change. "They are barrel racing. The object is to get your horse around the barrel and across the finish line in the shortest time."

"Like dressage, but no gates or jumping." Carina's expression didn't change. "They have bad form."

Lane chuckled. When it came to riding, English definitely had a more rigid posture than Western's loose one-handed reining. "Dressage and barrel racing are two very different competitive sports, but they have a lot of similarities, too. You know, I could show you around the rodeo school and we can even stop over at the hippotherapy center afterward and see some of their horses."

"Hippo?" Carina made eye contact with him for the first time during their conversation.

"Hippotherapy. It's where they utilize the horse's movements as a form of physical and occupational therapy to help people overcome disabilities and injuries."

"The horses help them?" Carina's face brightened.

"They sure do. What do you say I give you the grand tour?"

Carina looked toward the stables. "My mom really doesn't like you."

Lane followed Carina's gaze and saw Lucy watching them in the distance. "I wouldn't exactly say that."

"I would. And if she doesn't like you, then I like you."

Well, that figures. Do the exact opposite of what you think your mother wants. He guessed he could reason with her logic. He was fairly certain he'd done the same thing at her age.

Lane fought the urge to remind Carina her mother was experiencing the same learning curve she was. He feared by doing so he'd cause her to stop talking, and from what Lucy had told him yesterday, Carina hadn't done much talking to anyone lately. He found it impossible not to smile in Carina's presence. He hadn't met Lucy at that age, but knowing what he did about her and her family, he pictured her acting exactly the same way toward her mother.

"Listen, I'm sorry about your dad. I lost mine to cancer when I was ten. If you ever want to talk about it, I'm here. If not, that's fine. And before you ask, no, your mother did not put me up to saying that."

Carina held his gaze, not saying a word. He feared he had pushed her too far, too soon. "Can I meet the barrel racers?"

"Sure. Let's go." Lane gave Lucy a quick wave to reassure her Carina was all right. She didn't wave in return, just turned and walked away with her head down. Carina would probably cringe if she realized how much she and Lucy were alike.

He hadn't thought about it for years, but he hadn't felt as though he could confide in his mother, either, when his father had died. It'd been different for his mom. She'd watched his father battle cancer for a very long time and he would never forget what she said the morning he died. "It was a blessing... He's no longer in pain." As a ten-year-old who had just lost his father, Lane hadn't seen it as a blessing. It had been the worst thing imaginable. That was when he'd gotten involved with horses. He'd hung around the Ramble-wood Feed & Grain looking for odd jobs after school. Once he'd worked a few summers on a neighboring ranch, Curly hired him on at Bridle Dance. It hadn't hurt that his summer girlfriend stayed on the same ranch. As much as he felt he deserved Lucy's job, he didn't think it would be that easy to walk away from the place he'd cut his teeth on.

Lane introduced Carina to Sandra, the rodeo school's barrel racing instructor. He sat on the top fence rail as Sandra explained the sport. Carina met some of the racers, a few not much older than she was. The more she spoke about horses, the more her visible nervousness began to fade away. It gave Lane an idea. He'd have to run it by Lucy first, but he didn't see how she could say no. Then again, when it came to Lucy, nothing was logical. Including his renewed feelings toward her. He couldn't love her and he couldn't hate her, either. Somehow he didn't think the middle of the road would satisfy him.

Lucy hadn't considered the ramifications of seeing Lane with her daughter. No matter how hard she tried, she couldn't erase the vision of him with their son. She didn't regret having Carina, but she could've had both. She could've had her son *and* her daughter. The way it should have been. The way it would never be.

"Well, aren't you just as pretty as the day is long." The silhouette of a man formed in the entrance of the stables, the voice slightly familiar. "I heard you were back in town, breaking hearts all over again."

"Rusty?" Lucy said as his face came into view. "How are you?" She gave the older man a welcoming hug and kiss on both cheeks.

"I'm good. I creak a little more these days." Rusty twirled Lucy under his left hand the same way he used to when he'd taught her how to line dance many summers ago. "You grew up quite right, Miss Lucy. I'm sorry to hear about your husband's passing."

"Ex-husband, and thank you." That hadn't taken long to get around. "I see you've been talking to Lane."

"Don't you go fussin' at the man. I know because I nagged him last night."

"Oh, so you're the reason he showed up on my front porch." Lucy had to give it to the man. Probably well into his 70s and still wrapped up in other people's business. "It's nice to see you haven't lost your charm."

"I knew he'd end up your way. It was only a matter of time before you two ended up back together."

"Whoa!" Lucy stepped back. "Lane and I are not getting back together. I have a daughter now and she's my first priority. Work comes second and I come after that. There's no room in my life for Lane or any man, for that matter."

Rusty scratched his chin. "Far be it from me to tell you otherwise. What kind of trouble are you getting yourself into this morning?"

He gave up a little too easily on the matchmaking

to be believable. "It's been a while and I wanted to reacquaint myself with Western riding. I was hoping one of the grooms could give me a quick refresher course today."

"You don't need a groom for that," Rusty said. "You need a real cowboy to show you how it's done."

"If you're suggesting Lane teach me, the answer is no."

"I'm doing no such thing. I'm suggesting that I do the honors." The man bent slightly at the waist, one arm folded behind his back, the other splayed across his waist. "Is that how they do it where you come from?"

"Maybe if you were taking a curtain call." The gesture—however awkward—touched Lucy. Her shoulders sagged in relief. At least, she thought it was relief. The farther Lane was from her, the better. She needed to make that her new mantra. "You're not one of my employees, are you?"

"No, ma'am, I'm still out there riding the fence. Only nowadays we do it in a Jeep instead of on horseback. This ranch has gotten too big. How about we get you saddled up? We'll take my boy Kentucky for a spin."

"I remember him."

"Sometimes things don't change as much as you think they do."

Lucy had a strong suspicion there was more to Rusty's statement than just his horse, but she chose to ignore it.

"That's funny." Rusty stopped in front of a stall

containing a gorgeous American paint horse with bright ice-blue eyes. "Lane mentioned taking Frankie camping this weekend. I thought he'd be long gone by now."

The horse strode to the stall door, his head up in an attempt to catch her scent. Lucy moved closer and stroked the bridge of his nose. Frankie snorted and nodded approvingly at the gesture.

"Lane is with my daughter at the rodeo school." Lucy hadn't meant to take him away from his plans for the weekend. "Maybe we should do this some other time. I didn't know he was going camping. I should go get her."

"Girl, haven't you learned by now that Lane doesn't do anything he doesn't want to do?" Rusty unlatched Kentucky's stall door, slipped a nylon halter over his head and clipped a lead rope to it. "Your daughter will be fine. Lane's excellent with kids. There are so many of them on this ranch he's always showing one of them how to ride or do something. Carina is her name, right?"

"It is." She wasn't sure why it bothered her that Rusty had mentioned Lane was excellent with children. All these years she'd resolutely believed she'd married Antonio because Lane didn't want a family. Between last night and this morning, she'd heard the complete opposite. She couldn't help but wonder, if she'd been honest from the moment she discovered she was pregnant, if things would've been different. The doctor had told her the extra stress wasn't doing her baby any good, but she'd gone along with her family's plan and had married Antonio despite her love for Lane. Securing her child's future had trumped her heart.

"Lucy?" Rusty stood with Kentucky halfway down the stable corridor, waiting for her. "Are you coming?"

Lucy jogged to catch up to him. "I'm all yours."

"That's what all the ladies say," Rusty teased, throwing one lanky arm around her shoulders. "It gets better, kiddo. I promise. All I'm going to say is keep an open mind."

"About what?"

"Everything. Life. Work."

Lucy laughed. "Okay. I don't remember you being philosophical, but I promise to keep that in mind." As long as it didn't involve a trip down memory "Lane," she'd be good.

Chapter Five

Lane stood in the corridor outside his office Monday morning. Behind the partially open door, Lucy flipped frantically through a large book. *Is that a textbook?* He pushed the door open farther to get a better look, but she quickly slammed the book closed and jammed it into the tote bag at her feet. *New boots.* Well, they looked pretty used and abused. He suspected they were an old pair of Ella's. He hadn't meant to make her feel self-conscious about her clothes.

He hadn't seen Lucy again Saturday. He'd spent the majority of the day with Carina, until Ella called for her shortly before dinner. Ella had invited him to eat with them, but he didn't feel comfortable breaking bread in Nicolino's house after their conversation the other day. The only information Ella had volunteered about Lucy was that Rusty had become her tutor of sorts. He'd attempted to find out more from the old man, but Rusty hadn't said anything other than she'd done a good job. Rumor had it he'd given her another lesson on Sunday.

"I was hoping we'd have a chance to talk this morning." Lane sat at his desk across from her.

"I'm meeting with the farrier shortly," Lucy said without looking up. "The rest of my day is booked introducing myself personally to the rest of the employees."

He refused to allow her dismissive attitude to get the best of him. "Is this how it's going to be between us?"

Lucy sighed. "This is how it needs to be." She folded her hands. Her face softened slightly. "It may not be ideal or even what we both want, but you are my employee, and we need to respect that. We can't spend every day rehashing the past."

"As far as I'm concerned, we don't have a past anymore." He could be just as dismissive. "I wanted to discuss Carina."

"I appreciate the time you spent with my daughter on Saturday." Lucy hefted her bag onto the desk with a resounding thud. How many books did she have in there? "Rusty told me you had a camping trip planned and I wish you had mentioned it beforehand. I assure you my daughter will not be a bother ever again."

"What is wrong with you today? If this is about the kiss—"

"It's not. It's about me getting my priorities straight, and I'm sorry, but rekindling a romance with my boyfriend from ten years ago is not on the list. It hurts too much, Lane. My feelings for you are all over the place. And yes, I admit it—I still have feelings for you. But I think it's best if we keep our distance from one another unless it's business related. Now, if you'll excuse me."

Lucy stood cautiously, bracing her hands on the desk for support. When she caught him watching, she went ramrod straight, wincing at the same time. She grabbed a straw hat that he'd failed to notice earlier from the credenza and pulled it down low, shielding her eyes from him. Another castoff from Ella, he presumed. Slowly and rigidly, she made her way to the door.

"What's wrong, cowgirl? A little stiff? I didn't think an experienced rider like you would get saddle sore."

Lucy spun to face him—her eyes widening at the sudden movement. "For the record, my riding experience far exceeds anything you're aware of. I shouldn't have to justify myself, but for you I will. I haven't ridden in about two months. So yes, I'm sore today. But it's a good sore. And no matter how hard you try, you won't get the best of me."

"Actually, I hope I do, because everyone expects the best from you around here. For what it's worth, I'm glad Rusty was able to help you." Her walls were up and he knew he was partially responsible. "There's nothing wrong with admitting you need help."

Lucy ignored the comment. "I met with the night manager briefly this morning, and we've scheduled a meeting after work. I'd appreciate you joining us. I want to make sure we're all on the same page. Brad has some great ideas."

"That won't be possible. I can do it tomorrow, but

Mondays and Wednesdays are out. At least until the middle of December."

"Why?" She narrowed her eyes, as if expecting a phony excuse.

"I didn't have the privilege of earning my degree straight out of high school. I still have two years left until I get my bachelor's." Curly and Nicolino had always worked around his college schedule. Usually it didn't affect his job, but there were times when he needed to take exams during the day and no one thought twice about it. He'd always made sure someone covered for him and he'd even come back to work late at night if he'd needed to. "I've never missed a single class and I don't intend on missing tonight, either."

"You're in college?" Lucy asked. The stupefied look on her face insulted Lane. "What are you majoring in?"

"Business management."

"Are you minoring in anything? Like equine science?"

"No, I hope to someday follow in your cousin's footsteps." He resented being put on the defensive. "I'll work my way up the ladder the same way he did when he went to night school." Lucy blinked twice at his statement, as if it had been the first time she'd heard mention of it. "I can stay up-to-date on the latest equine science discoveries and technology through our veterinarians and breed managers. My vision for Bridle Dance is to employ the best people in multiple fields to ensure the highest quality horses."

"I'm glad you're continuing with your education." Lucy inched toward the door with her heavy bag. "I'll fill you in tomorrow on my meeting with Brad."

Lane couldn't help but notice how carefully calculated Lucy's movements were. "There was once a time when your cousin actually liked me." Lane knew he should feel sorry for her, but he didn't. It went along with learning the job and she had to pull her weight, too. "When Cole rehired me after I returned from Wyoming, Nicolino didn't seem too pleased. He's never acted hostile toward me, but he hasn't exactly been friendly, either. Once he became general operations manager, we didn't have much to do with one another. I always answered to Curly. It's not an obvious dislike, but it's definitely there. I'd ask you to find out how I got on his bad side, but that would be violating our employee-employer relationship."

Lucy stared at him for a moment and then began to hobble away.

"You know what's good for sore muscles?" He couldn't resist one final tease.

Lucy froze, not bothering to turn around. "Let me guess—a massage by none other than yours truly."

Lane snorted, enjoying the vision that immediately came to mind. "No, I was thinking more along the lines of Rusty's homemade liniment. Ask him about it."

Lane saw Lucy's back stiffening and imagined how red her face must be.

"I'm fine," she growled and awkwardly continued down the stable corridor.

"I'm sure you are, but if you need something to soothe your muscles, he's your man."

Lucy stopped in front of one of the stalls and peered into it. "I almost forgot." A slow smile spread across her face as she turned to him. "I have a meeting with the grooms this morning, so they'll be busy. I don't want us to get off schedule, so I'll need you to muck this entire row for me."

He couldn't argue with her. She was the boss. He should have seen that one coming, though. A groom brought over a wheelbarrow and handed him a shovel. "Have fun," the groom said before catching up with Lucy, who waved goodbye over her shoulder.

"Well played," Lane mumbled. Here he'd thought the job would get the best of Lucy, and she was getting the best of him.

FOR THE LOVE of all things holy. Lucy couldn't remember ever being this sore. She eased down onto a hay bale while Jorge finished trimming the hoof on a mare. It probably wouldn't have been so bad if she hadn't fallen off Kentucky. Rusty had been relentless with her lessons on Sunday. She'd expected a one- or two-hour refresher course on Western saddling and riding; instead she'd apparently enrolled in cutting-horse boot camp. She'd never been more scared and fascinated at the same time.

As a hunter jumper for the past ten years, she was used to having complete control of the horse. She still had some control, but not nearly as much as she wanted. Kentucky had been trained to read cattle.

She hadn't. Regardless of how hard she tried, she kept stiffening up and leaning in the saddle, knocking her off balance. She was grateful for the lessons, but it wasn't as though she'd be out there training the horses. Was it?

"Did Curly train any of the cutting horses?" Lucy asked Jorge.

His rasp stilled and then continued its long strokes along the hoof's underside. "Yes, all the time."

Lucy's stomach tightened. "But Bridle Dance employs trainers." Surely if she had been expected to train cutting horses, Nicolino would've said something. Then again, he hadn't told her about Lane, either.

"They do. Sometimes we don't have as many as they'd like, or somebody's on vacation. This is a big ranch."

Lucy wished people would stop reminding her of that fact. "I'm assuming Lane also trains."

"Yes. He's very good. Curly taught him everything he knew."

Great, Jorge was a Lane supporter, too. Wasn't everybody? He lowered the mare's foot from the hoof jack and handed the lead rope off to a waiting groom. Lucy flipped through her notepad, anxious to begin their meeting so she could discover what other surprises the job entailed.

"Are you sure you're up for this?"

Lucy opened her mouth to argue and then quickly shut it. Jorge's tone hadn't been accusatory or demeaning in any way. He actually sounded concerned.

"No, I'm not sure. But I have faith in my cousin and he wouldn't have hired me if he didn't think I could handle it."

She couldn't have been any more honest. Being barn manager had quickly become one of the biggest challenges she'd faced in life. She refused to run from it. She might not have the strength and ability yet, but she'd find both.

"Then I wish you the best."

Lucy liked Jorge. She appreciated his sincerity in contrast to Lane's judgmental "I can do this job better than you" approach.

By the end of the day, Lucy felt accomplished for the first time since she'd arrived. She'd successfully met with almost every employee, heard some of their grievances and suggestions, and implemented a few small changes of her own. Carina had visited briefly after school but hadn't had much to say when she'd asked how her day had gone.

Lucy's conversation with the school earlier hadn't gone as smoothly as she'd anticipated. She'd asked if the teachers would mind writing out Carina's homework assignments and discovered Carina had been argumentative and adamant she didn't need extra help. Tonight she planned to go through her backpack and see the assignments. She almost didn't want to go home. She loved Carina more than life itself, but she wasn't looking forward to another epic battle.

"Have a good night." Lane popped his head in the office door. "I'm heading out. Is there anything you need before I go?"

Lucy almost didn't know how to respond to his civility. "No, I'm great. Enjoy your evening."

Maybe there was hope for a decent working relationship between them. She admired Lane for continuing his education. Lane had implied earlier that she was privileged to have gone to college, but her education had come at a price. Carina's nannies had heard her first words. They'd helped her take her first steps. They'd fed her and changed her more than Lucy had. Wanting to be the best possible person for her daughter drove her then and still did. She'd made sacrifices, maybe even too many, but her schooling had given her something to fall back on when Antonio died. Contrary to Lane's assumption, it hadn't been easy. Her final year of higher secondary school had been delayed almost two years because of her pregnancy complications.

"Lucy!" Lane bellowed from the corridor.

Lucy trudged out of the office. Her muscles felt a little more limber this afternoon after some strategic yoga stretches at lunchtime. "You called?"

"Fearless isn't in the correct stall. Neither is Pluto or Amaze Yourself." Lane stopped a nearby groom. "Why are these horses in the wrong stall?"

The young groom couldn't have been more than seventeen or eighteen years old. He was visibly shaken by Lane's tone. Now she understood what Nicolino meant about Lane's lack of polish with the employees.

Lucy stepped between them. "Your name's Peter, right? You're the new hire. We're both new hires."

Lucy turned to Lane. "It's his first day. Let's move the horses to the proper stalls instead of getting upset."

Lane stormed to one of the stall doors. "Do you see this card?" Lucy wasn't sure if he was directing the question at her or Peter. They'd discuss the cards on Thursday. "It has the horse's name and turnout-pasture location. I can't even begin to stress how important it is for the correct horse to make it into the proper stall. Every card has a corresponding number matching a specific feed and medication schedule. Sudden changes in a horse's diet can cause colic. If I hadn't caught this, we could've had a serious problem."

"They haven't been fed yet." Lucy checked each of the feed buckets. "It's okay, Lane—we caught it in time. I'm sure Peter understands he needs to be more careful."

"Excuse me." Peter wrung his hands. "I don't understand what I did wrong. The tall guy with the red hair told me to match pasture numbers to the stall cards. That's what I did."

"Oh no." Lucy swallowed hard. "It's my fault."

"What?" Lane asked.

"Peter, it's okay—you can go." The kid ran out the front entrance so fast she doubted he'd be back tomorrow. "There was an excessive amount of standing water in one of the pastures. A few of the ranch hands helped me look for the source, but we couldn't locate one. I couldn't tell if it leached from underground, but it appears to have happened rapidly. It was too risky leaving the horses there not knowing what bacteria could be in the water. I was trying to avoid grease heel, so I transferred them to a dry pasture."

Lane rubbed his eyes. "You did the right thing, but you can't move horses without following procedure. We have too many to keep track of."

"I take full responsibility for it. I also see a major flaw in the system. Many of the halters don't have the horses' names on them. That alone would be an excellent double check. Even if we write them on with a Sharpie. And look at these photos." Lucy poked at the curled edges of a faded ink-jet print taped to the front of a stall. "These need to be replaced with new photos and some form of a protective cover over them like the breeding wing does. I also noticed that the stable-management software seems to be very up-to-date on the breeding horses, but not on the cutters in training. There's no consistency, which boggles my mind for a place this large." Lucy couldn't resist the subtle dig about the ranch's size.

Lane continued down the corridor, checking every horse. "This one's in the wrong stall, too." Lane removed his phone from his back pocket and called the feed room. "Hold off on feeding and meds. The new kid put the horses in the wrong stalls. I'll call you once I have it straightened out."

Lucy remembered seeing a digital camera in one of the office filing cabinets. She retrieved it along with her laptop. "I might as well start photographing this row now. Why did you blame it on the groom? It was my fault."

"Nobody else needs to know that and I can pretty

much promise that kid isn't coming back." Lane tried
to squeeze past her in the doorway, causing his chest
to graze hers. He hesitated, staring down at her before continuing. Her skin prickled at his brief touch,
annoying her further.

Lucy cleared her throat. "I don't need you cover-
ing for me. I made the mistake, but we need to correct the system. Curly shouldn't have been so lax on
something this critical. Why was a new employee
doing a job that clearly took somebody with more
knowledge to handle?"

Lane closed the office door. "He was your responsibility. You knew it was his first day. Who did you
think he answered to?"

"I—I don't know." The thought hadn't dawned
on her that morning. She didn't even know who had
hired him. "I guess I assumed you or a head groom.
Peter said he was only doing what he was told."

"That's another issue I—you—need to handle. The
tall guy with the red hair is Dale. Find out what happened from him."

"Understood." She wished Lane had acknowledged
Curly's lapse in horse identification. He might very
well have known each horse by name, but everyone
else didn't. As for Peter, she knew he was one of
her employees, so why hadn't she taken charge? Unfortunately, she already knew the answer. She was
overwhelmed and underqualified. "I'll handle this.
Go to class."

"No, this is too important for me to walk away

from and you don't know these horses." At least they finally agreed on something.

"I need to call Ella and ask her to watch Carina for a few more hours." Her muscles tensed. Lucy had made similar phone calls all of her daughter's life. School used to be her excuse for coming home late; now it was work. She needed to do whatever it took to prevent late hours from becoming a habit again. Carina deserved to have her one remaining parent home every night. Anything less was unacceptable.

"You take the photos. I'll print and add them to the database," Lane said. "It will go twice as fast that way. For what it's worth, Cole Langtry told me over a week ago that he'd hired a new groom and I completely forgot about it. Granted, it's technically your job to oversee the new hire, but you wouldn't have known unless I told you. So this is on me tonight. One of the owners entrusted me with the job and I blew it."

Lane's admission caught Lucy off guard. She wanted to thank him, but somehow that didn't seem adequate, especially when he'd made a point to tell her earlier that he'd never missed a class. Lane was more of a stand-up guy than she'd given him credit for. The teenager she'd fallen in love with had grown into a man she could easily envision herself dating. If it hadn't been for their past and present situations, she would have embraced the possibility. Now she could only lock the thought away, deep in her heart along with the rest of him.

BY THE BEGINNING of the following week, Lane needed to formulate a new strategy. His own job had suffered because he'd been too busy helping Lucy. After ordering supplies had taken twice the usual time two days in a row, he decided it was easier to do it himself rather than explain each step. The same went for scheduling Coggins reports—which the state required to ensure each horse had been tested for equine infectious anemia before transport—and double-checking time cards. She still wasn't familiar enough with the employees to know which ones had the propensity to falsify their time cards. Dale had been a prime example last week when he'd asked someone else to punch him out long after he'd left for the day.

"I don't agree." Lucy sat at her desk, the telephone receiver in one hand, a pen wildly tapping in the other. "She doesn't need to be left back—she needs extra help. Why can't you provide that?"

Lane hadn't meant to eavesdrop on her conversation, but it was next to impossible not to considering the amount of time she spent on the phone with Carina's school. If he hadn't been so tired of the constant distraction, he might actually have felt more compassion about the situation.

"Merda!" Lucy swore in Italian, slamming down the phone. "That was the school. Carina went from the best in her class in Italy to a kid who doesn't apply herself here. I know it's only been a week, but I'm afraid it's just going to get worse. She wants to go back to Italy in the worst way."

Lane grabbed the farrier binder off the shelf and

noticed Lucy hadn't printed or filed the past few days' reports. Slowly exhaling, he sat at his desk and searched his email for the reports so he could print them himself. "I'm not sure if you're asking for my advice or not, but have you discussed this with Ella? She always seems to be mother of the year."

Lucy leaned back in her chair. "She makes it look so effortless, even with five children." She reached behind her and took the pages he'd printed. "She says Carina needs time and I'm inclined to believe her. Pushing her to a lower grade is not the right solution. She can do the work. She needs to apply herself instead of rebelling against me." Lucy began to hand him the pages, then realized what they were. "Why are you printing these?"

"I needed to see today's schedule and saw you hadn't done it yet. No big deal. Thought I would do you a favor."

"Are you insinuating I'm not doing my job?" Lucy cocked her head.

"No, I think you're a bit overwhelmed." Lane carefully controlled his tone. "And as your assistant, I'm helping you."

"Thanks, but I've already printed them." Lucy picked up a binder from the far corner of the desk and passed it to him. "If you had asked, I would have told that I started a new binder because that one was too full. I appreciate the confidence, though."

Lane couldn't have felt worse if he tried. "You're right—I assumed the worst. I apologize." He took the binder and radioed the names to one of the grooms before tossing the pages he'd printed into the recycling bin.

Somehow Lucy had managed to handle everything he'd thrown her way. That wasn't to say they hadn't experienced some setbacks. Regardless of how long it took her to complete a task, she did it. At what cost, though?

A big part of him wondered if moving here had been in Carina's best interests. He understood Lucy's need to provide for her daughter, but he couldn't wrap his head around why she'd taken such a drastic step. If his mother had moved him to a new town—never mind a new country—away from everything he'd known after his father's death, he probably would've rebelled ten times more than Carina.

Lane didn't have time to hang around and discuss it with her. He had a statistics exam tonight and he could not afford to miss class again. He'd already put out feelers for a new job. He hoped with Curly's help, one would come sooner rather than later. Now he wondered if he'd been too hasty. He saw the potential for Lucy's frustration with Carina to send her packing back to Italy. The thought alone should have given him cause for celebration. It didn't. Instead it constricted his heart.

I'm in trouble.

Chapter Six

When Friday afternoon finally arrived, Lucy couldn't wait for the weekend. Even though it meant more time risking her life on the back of a horse, she craved the challenge. Her lessons were new and exciting, allowing her the luxury to concentrate on just one thing. She needed a distraction from Lane, above all else. The more time she spent around him, the more memories she realized she'd forgotten. It saddened her in a way. Not because of Lane, but because of Antonio. He'd been wonderful to her during their marriage and even afterward. She hoped the day would never come that she lost any of the memories they'd shared.

When Nicolino had offered her the job, she'd immediately jumped on it, believing the change would be better for Carina. Now she wasn't so sure. She didn't want her daughter to forget the little things—subtle memories that were easily recalled when you saw something familiar…and she'd taken the familiar away. More and more she noticed Carina desperately attempting to hold on to her father. It had begun with the locket around her neck containing his photo. Then

Lucy noticed a few photos in her bedroom, followed by the one she found in her backpack. The other day when she came home from work, his picture was on the refrigerator, and this morning she'd noticed one in the living room.

Even after they'd divorced, Lucy hadn't put away his photos. He'd always be Carina's father, and when they'd moved to Texas, the box containing his photos should have been the first one they had unpacked... together. She should have been more aware of her daughter's pain.

Lucy picked up her reports from the breed manager's office. While she loved her job for the most part, equine artificial insemination fascinated her even more. She'd seen two foals born this week, and she hated that the majority of the deliveries occurred at night. They always notified her before each birth, but leaving Carina alone in the middle of the night was not an option. Carina already had a difficult enough time in school, so being woken up in the night wouldn't do her any favors, either. Lucy hoped her daughter would have the opportunity to witness a foaling soon.

Lucy exited through the side door of the stables and waited for Carina. She watched her barrel down the main ranch road ahead of her cousins. If Lucy hadn't been standing there, she doubted she would have even stopped to say hello.

"I got paid today and I thought we could go out to dinner and do some shopping afterward," Lucy said.

Carina shrugged, seemingly more interested in

the riders at the rodeo school. She'd become more despondent during the past week and her grades had continued to slip.

"Can I get cowgirl boots?" she asked without looking away from the school.

The question surprised Lucy. "Of course you can." She wanted to ask why her daughter had changed her mind about Western riding, but she didn't want to jinx it. "We can go to the place in town where I bought my first pair. I'll even let you pick the restaurant, too."

"The girls at school always talk about a Cajun place. Can we go there?"

"We'll go anyplace you'd like." How exciting! Her daughter had finally made friends. "Do you want to invite your friends to the ranch this weekend?"

"They're already here," Carina scoffed. "Can I go now?"

Lucy nodded. The "girls at school" were the rodeo-school girls, not Carina's classmates. Carina had begun hanging around the barrel racers instead of walking to Ella's with her cousins after school. Lucy still hadn't decided if that was good or bad. She allowed it because most of the kids were Carina's age, but she didn't want them to be her daughter's only friends, either. She hated questioning every parental decision she made lately. Lucy checked her watch. She had two more horses to bathe. She'd implemented a short-term program where she worked alongside her employees two days a week to gain a better understanding of their responsibilities. She did the same jobs they did, and so far it had worked beautifully. More of the managers needed cross-training in the event of an emergency.

Unfortunately, Lane had balked at his inclusion in her plan, informing Lucy he'd worked every job under him on his way up the ladder to assistant barn manager. He hadn't been nasty about it, and he could've mentioned his almost promotion, but he hadn't. Despite their differences, he'd been more helpful than she'd expected or even deserved.

Lucy's doubts in her own abilities had faded some during her second week on the ranch. Curly had been one of those rare employers whom everybody loved. As wonderful as he'd been, he hadn't been exactly thorough when it came to documenting procedures and job descriptions. Lane had begun the daunting task after Curly had left. Lucy had a hunch he'd waited to spare the old-timer's feelings. That was something she could always say about Lane: he put everyone else first.

Lucy sighed. Would he have put their child first if he had known? She'd stopped asking those questions when she'd miscarried their son. Now she asked them every day. She wanted to relieve the burden she bore and tell him the truth. He thought he had the answers, but they weren't the right ones. A part of her felt he deserved the truth and the other part said telling him the truth was selfish. He already detested what she'd done, but he'd hate the reality even more. She wanted to spare him the grief of losing a child he'd never even known about. If he never spoke to her again, she'd survive. But she refused to let him doubt himself or wonder whether if he'd said or done things differently before she left for Italy they might have had a different outcome. She'd lived with that self-doubt for ten years. Some days it had been all-consuming. She didn't wish that feeling on anybody. No, things were fine the way they were. What he didn't know wouldn't hurt him.

LANE KNEW HE would find Lucy either in or near the breeding wing. It was where she belonged. Her master's degree in equine science was more suited to breed management and he believed it was where her heart was. The last thing he needed was to worry about her heart. He had a hard enough time keeping track of his own.

"Would you mind reviewing next week's employee schedule before I post it?" Technically, he didn't need her approval, but he wanted her to get familiar with the procedure since it was really her job.

"Sure." Lucy ran her finger down the list of names. "I thought Tracy was on vacation next week, and double-check with Rob about Thursday and Friday. He mentioned his mom was having surgery. You may need to reschedule him. It sounded pretty serious and I think he wants to be at the hospital that day."

Lane didn't know what to say except "Good catch." Her personal knowledge of the employees impressed him. It shouldn't have, though. She'd always been very personable and outgoing. She had succeeded in separating their past from the present and he was still struggling to do so.

"Great job, Lucy," Cole said as he passed by. "I love the cross-training idea. I don't know how you manage to get it all done."

You've got to be kidding me.

"Thank you." Lucy turned to Lane. "See, I'm getting there." She beamed. "I know you still have doubts about my ability to do this job, but I'm determined to prove myself."

Lane didn't want to tell her the only reason she'd been able to spend this much time with everyone was because he'd picked up the slack. He hated doing double the work, but her crash course had been a necessity. He just hoped it didn't go to her head and lead her to think she knew everything about everybody's jobs. One day shadowing someone didn't make a person proficient. He also didn't appreciate her taking over the policies-and-procedures project he'd been working on. She could've at least offered to work with him on it.

"I will admit, I have fewer doubts than I had before." It wasn't a lie; he did have fewer doubts. He still doubted she'd last, especially if he wasn't around to help her. "I'll make these changes and post the schedule."

The walls of the breeding corridor began to suffocate him. Compared to the other wings, this one had far less traffic and noise. He had a million thoughts he wanted to share running through his mind. Every night, he laid in bed remembering all the people they'd both known. He wanted to catch her up on their lives and tell her about the new businesses that had come and gone in town. He wanted to take her dancing at Slater's Mill just to prove some things stayed the same no matter how much time passed.

"Great—thank you." Lucy gave his hand a gentle squeeze as she passed him, surprising them both. It was a casual gesture she'd done a thousand times when they were kids. "Lane—I'm sorry. I didn't mean—I shouldn't have done that."

Lane couldn't help himself. He smiled. Big. "I guess old habits really are hard to forget. Don't give it a second thought." *Give it many second thoughts.* "I need to get back to work."

"Me, too." Lucy held her paperwork tight to her chest and quickly walked away, allowing him the pleasure of watching her leave. Maybe she hadn't separated work from the past as successfully as he'd thought.

LANE LED TWO cutting horses to the rodeo school before he left for the day. The Langtrys had always conducted cutting-horse workshops and seminars, but this year they had added week-long clinics to their roster.

He'd noticed Carina perched in her usual spot on the fence when he'd dropped the horses off. A half hour later, she hadn't moved an inch.

"We have to stop meeting like this," Lane said as he joined her at the rail.

"Are you stalking me?" Carina giggled.

"Stalking?" Lane laughed, enjoying her smile. "I see somebody's English has improved."

"I heard a cowgirl ask a cowboy that the other day."

Lane didn't know if he should be amused or terrified at her statement.

"You really love the barrel racers, don't you?" Lane still hadn't spoken to Lucy about his idea. After the way she'd bitten his head off the first time he'd attempted to, he hadn't felt much like trying again. Earlier in the hallway would've been the perfect time.

Carina's smile brightened. "It looks like they're flying."

"How would you like to take lessons?" Lane asked.

She hopped off the fence rail and began jumping up and down. "Really? I want to so bad."

"Whoa! Wait a minute, you two." Lucy startled them both. "Don't you think you should have asked my permission first?"

"Mamma, please!" Carina pleaded. "You ride English and Western—why can't I?"

"Because we can't afford lessons right now and I don't know the first thing about barrel racing to be able to teach you myself," Lucy said. "What about your dressage training? Are you going to let it all go to waste?"

"Actually, she can do both."

Lucy glared at him. "Lane, we can't afford it. Why are you doing this?"

"If you would stop a minute and listen to me, I'll explain." Lane had gone from having no women to deal with to trying to figure out two… Well, one and a half. "One of the barrel-racing instructors also teaches Western dressage at another facility. Carina would have the option—"

"Honey." Lucy cut him off. "Do Mamma a favor. Call Ella and ask what time we're meeting them later for family game night."

Carina rolled her eyes, clearly not buying her mother's stall tactic. Lucy practically dragged Lane into the bushes so they were out of Carina's view. "You're getting her hopes up and I can't afford to follow through. I can barely afford to buy her new boots and take her to dinner tonight." Lucy's carefully practiced American accent faded with each syllable. "You're making me look bad in front of my child."

Lane closed what distance remained between them. The rest of the ranch didn't need to hear Lucy berating him. It had been difficult enough keeping his head up among the whispers when he'd lost the barn manager position. He didn't need people talking about his public scolding by his new boss.

"I tried to discuss this with you last week, but you never gave me the chance. Instead you assumed I wanted to talk about us." Lane lowered his voice. She was trying to do right by her daughter and he didn't want to appear heartless. "I know you're working hard to prove yourself here and at home, but don't you see how much her demeanor changes when she's around the rodeo-school kids?"

"It's all she's talked about." Lucy peered through the bushes at Carina talking on the phone. "Antonio gave her whatever she asked for. She never demanded anything—it was always within reason. She's a good kid who wants her life back and I can't give it to her." Lucy looked up at him. "Then you swoop in and dangle a carrot in front of her and I have to tell her no. I'm the bad guy again. Thanks."

Lane reached for her hand, but she immediately pulled away, folding her arms tightly across her chest. He cursed himself for the constant need to comfort her. Especially when he was at fault.

"I was outside yesterday when the bus dropped the kids off after school. Carina ran down that main road and beelined straight for the barrel-racing corral. You should've seen the smile on her face."

"I saw it earlier." Lucy shook her head. "Her smile's a rarity these days. I've actually had to look at photographs to remind myself how happy she used to be."

"Then let her be happy." Lane tilted back his hat. "You don't need to buy anything. She can borrow a horse and saddle the same way the other kids do around here. All she needs to do is show up. I will take care of the rest."

"Oh no." Lucy stepped away from him. "I'm not allowing you to pay for my daughter's riding lessons."

"And I won't be," Lane said. "Before she can even decide if she wants to barrel-race or try Western dressage, she needs to learn the basics. I've trained many kids to ride. I can teach her speed and discipline and at least get her to the point where she's proficient enough to move on to one of the rodeo-school instructors. By then you'll be on your feet and able to swing the lessons. And if for some reason you can't, then we'll discuss it. Will you let me do this for her? You don't even need to be there."

"Ella said the usual time," Carina ground out behind them. "Are you two finished talking about me?"

Lucy pursed her lips. Her eyes darted between him and Carina. He wasn't sure if she'd explode or belt him. Either way, it didn't make an attractive picture.

"Let's hold off on the rodeo school," Lucy said. A tiny muscle along Carina's jawline pulsated. No child should feel that much tension. "At least for now." Carina's brows rose slightly. "Lane's offered to teach you how to ride Western. You've never even tried it, so let's see how you do and how you feel about it before we make any other plans."

Carina flung her arms around Lucy. *"Grazie, Mamma. Ti amo, ti amo, ti amo!"*

Lucy enveloped her tighter, kissing the top of her head. "You're welcome, *mia gattina*. I love you, too!" Her eyes shone with wetness as she met Lane's and mouthed, *Thank you*.

He nodded in response and headed toward the stables, allowing them time alone. It had been bad enough when one Italian cowgirl had gotten under his skin. Now he had two of them to contend with. Somehow their happiness had become a priority to him. And that was when he knew he was falling in love all over again.

Lucy hadn't seen Carina this excited since before the divorce. She'd told everyone who would listen at Cowpoke's Western Wear about the barrel racers. By the time they reached the Ragin' Cajun, Carina was hoarse from talking so much. Lucy loved her enthusiasm, but why couldn't she have chosen the safer Western dressage?

Lane had taken Lucy to a rodeo once. It was where they'd shared their first official kiss. She couldn't remember what event they'd been watching, but she'd never forget the way he'd made her feel that night. It wasn't just her first kiss with Lane; it had been *her first kiss*.

"Mamma, why are you smiling?" Carina dragged her back to the present. "Look!" She pointed to the bar area. "There's Lane. Can he eat with us?"

Lucy turned and saw Lane in a fresh pair of jeans and a brown plaid snap-front Western shirt. "I think he might be waiting for someone." And that thought bothered her.

Carina jumped off her chair and ran to him, practically knocking his drink over once she reached the bar.

Lucy took a two-second composure break before she chased after her daughter. "I apologize. She's really geared up tonight."

"That's okay." Lane's slow, easy grin and inviting dark chocolate eyes were almost too much temptation to bear. If this had been any other time and any other place, she'd probably have given in to the attraction and kissed him until the sun came up.

"Look." Carina twirled in front of him. "I got new boots. Now I'm ready to ride with you."

"You've created a monster," Lucy said.

"Come to our table," Carina interrupted, tugging on Lane's hand.

Lucy attempted to playfully cover Carina's mouth with her hand but she squirmed out of her grasp. "I already told you, I think he's meeting someone." He looked too good to be dining alone. "I'm—"

"I'm not meeting anyone." Lane slid from the high barstool chair, leaving mere inches between them. "I'd love to join you."

Oh. My. God. She inhaled him. Crisp, clean and oh so memorable. Their first kiss, last kiss and every passionate moment in between flashed vividly in her mind like a movie montage.

"Come on." Carina grabbed both of their hands, pulling them toward the table. "Tell me more about the barrel racers."

"We need to discuss that further." Lucy struggled to remain in the present. Lane pulled out her chair— a customary gesture she found extremely intimate tonight. "Thank you. Before she gets her heart even more set on barrel racing, I need a few questions answered. Starting with how safe is it? It looks insanely reckless."

"I've never seen anyone get hurt," Carina answered for him.

"You've watch experienced riders for a couple hours a day. I'm sure all of them have been injured at some point in their careers. Which happen to be very short, by the way." Lucy cautioned.

"If they are experienced, why are they in school?" Carina challenged.

Lane leaned back in his chair, laughing as he rubbed his palms across the tops of his thighs. She'd almost forgotten about his left-side dimple. One more item to add to his devilishly tempting good looks. He was the forbidden fruit she didn't need to taste.

"What is so funny?" Lucy asked.

"She's you. She's curious and fearless, the same way you were." Lucy's pulse quickened at the revelation.

"Tell me about my mamma when she was my age," Carina pleaded.

"We didn't know each other then." Lucy handed her a menu. "Why don't we figure out what to order instead?"

Lane set his menu on the table. "I met your mom when we were both fourteen."

Lucy shook her head in warning. He winked in response, not helping matters.

"Was she pretty?"

If Lane's reddened cheeks were any indication, Carina had gotten to him.

"Honey, stop asking so many questions." She felt a sting of heat rising to her own cheeks. A part of Lucy feared what he might say; the other couldn't wait for him to respond.

"Your mom—" Lane leaned across the table and

whispered "—is still as beautiful today as she was the day we met."

Be still, my beating heart. It was one thing to work with the man, but laughing and joking at the table, publicly in a restaurant like a family...it felt too real... too perfect...and impossible.

Chapter Seven

"Mamma." Lucy abruptly woke from a deliciously deep sleep. "Mamma, wake up." Carina continued to shake her.

Lucy sat upright, pulling her daughter close. "What is it, *mia gattina*?" She could barely make out her daughter's figure in the darkened room. "What time is it?" She peered at the clock on the nightstand. "You woke me up at five o'clock on my day off? What's wrong with you?" Lucy collapsed back onto the bed.

"Mamma, come on. We have to get ready." Carina tugged the covers off her and turned on the bedside lamp.

Lucy shivered. The room was chillier than when she had gone to bed. "Give me those. Ready for what?" She squinted against the offending light. "Turn that off, please."

"My lessons." Carina pursed her lips together, her hands sternly on her hips. That was when Lucy noticed she was already dressed.

Lucy reached over, flicked off the light herself and grabbed Carina, tucking her beneath the covers.

"We have a few more hours. I'm sure Lane isn't even awake." Then again, if his night had gone anything like hers, he'd lain awake thinking of her the same way she'd thought of him most of the night.

She'd enjoyed their dinner. A little too much. She couldn't remember the last time she'd felt that free. For a few hours, she hadn't worried about money or her job. Carina's school and the move from Italy had buried their ugly heads for a while. It had been peaceful. She'd actually relaxed and enjoyed herself.

"I thought all cowboys got up with the sun," Carina said.

"The sun isn't even up," Lucy groaned.

"Can I watch your lessons?"

Now she was awake. "Absolutely not." The last thing she needed was her daughter wanting to learn how to ride cutting horses. It was one thing to race across a dirt corral by yourself. There was no way she'd allow her daughter on the back of a cutting horse, surrounded by cattle. "Both of our lessons are at the same time, in different areas on the ranch. If you watched my lesson, you'd miss your own. You wouldn't want that, would you?"

"No." Carina sighed dramatically. "I guess not."

"You're not going to let me sleep, are you?" Lucy was almost afraid to get out of bed. Her moody daughter had almost returned to her normal bubbly self. There had been a few times during dinner when she'd caught Carina trying to figure out the exchanges between her and Lane. It had been natural curiosity more than anything, but Lucy had been aware of it.

"I'm nervous."

Lucy pulled her daughter closer. "You're a very accomplished rider. Lane's not going to ask you to do anything you're not ready to do. But you need to listen to everything he says."

"Do you think I'll ever be as good as them?"

"Who—the barrel racers?" Lucy sat up against the headboard. "You of all people know how much practice and dedication goes into an equestrian sport. You're not going to get on that horse today and ride like them. I'm sure they put in just as much time barrel-racing as you have in dressage."

"It looks a lot easier." Carina fiddled with a button on her shirt. "They don't have all the rules."

"They still have rules." Lucy brushed Carina's hair out of her eyes with her fingers. "What's the real reason you want to barrel race? Did somebody say something to you in school?"

Carina pulled away, slid off the other side of the bed and headed for the door. And up went the wall. It didn't take much to trigger it. Lucy would mention it to Lane and Ella later since her daughter seemed to open up to them much easier. Lucy's biggest concern was Carina's almost immediate attachment to Lane. She feared she was using him to fill the void left by Antonio. She'd rather Carina lean on Nicolino instead. It was safer, for both of their hearts.

Lucy double-checked the clock. She couldn't believe she was up this early without a valid reason. She stepped into her slippers and padded through the house to the kitchen. Carina sat cross-legged on the couch watching cartoons. Well, that was an improve-ment over a locked bedroom door. Progress.

She rinsed out the carafe and refilled the coffeepot. Back home in Italy, she'd had a staff to do it for her. The surprising part was she didn't miss it. She liked doing things for herself and Carina. Some days were harder than others, but everything they did together meant more. That is, when she had the time. She'd worked late every day except last night. Ella had been generously picking Carina up from the stables, feed-ing her dinner and helping her with homework, saying she was used to Nicolino coming home after the kids were already in bed. Those hours might have been fine for her cousin, but they weren't for her. She'd expected to be home early enough to have dinner with her child and go over her schoolwork together. It wasn't the only reason she felt guilty.

Her divorce from Antonio had been amicable. They'd both wanted to move on with their lives and find the people they were meant to be with. But for some reason, she felt guilty for enjoying herself with Lane. *Because you haven't told him the truth.*

"I can't. I just can't."

"Who are you talking to?" Carina asked from the living room.

Lucy squared her shoulders. "How about waffles for breakfast? I know the best place in town."

LANE GRABBED HIS keys and headed out the door. He'd been up and dressed for the past two hours. Quarter to six and he hadn't slept more than ten minutes at a time all night. He'd flirted with Lucy at dinner. He shouldn't have, but he had. And once he'd started, he hadn't known how to stop. Of course, it had all been innocent since Carina had been with them, but damned if it hadn't felt good. He'd never dated anyone with a kid—not that he and Lucy were dating or would date, although the thought had crossed his mind repeatedly once he'd arrived back at the bunkhouse.

That nervous flutter deep in the belly that women talked about…yeah, he had that. His mom affectionately referred to it as the lovebug and he'd been infected only once before. He started his truck, not wanting to keep his breakfast date waiting. She was the one person in his life who knew what he'd gone through when Lucy walked out of his life the first time. He needed her advice before he risked it happening a second time.

Ten minutes later, he braked in front of his mom's apartment. She was a chronic insomniac, so he'd known she'd be awake when he texted her at four in the morning. Barbara Morgan stepped onto the sidewalk just as he opened the passenger door for her.

"This is a pleasant surprise." She reached up and gave him a kiss on the cheek. "I don't see enough of you," she said as she climbed into the truck.

Lane closed the door and chuckled. It never took long for a mom guilt trip. "I can't remember why we stopped going to breakfast Saturday mornings." Lane slid in beside her. "It's been what, a year? We need to start doing this on a regular basis again."

"You won't get any arguments from me." They drove in silence for a few minutes before Lane felt his mother's stare.

Slowly, he turned toward her. "What?"

She shrugged. "Oh, nothing. I'm just waiting for you to tell me Lucy Travisonno is back in town."

"So you've heard." Lane gripped the steering wheel.

"I heard over two weeks ago. I also heard she has a kid. Is that what this breakfast is about? Are you going to tell me I'm a grandma?"

Lane braked in the middle of the street. "Mom!" He looked at her square in the face. "If Carina was my daughter, believe me, you would've been the second person to find out about it. She's not. But I am giving her riding lessons today and I kind of sort of had a dinner date with Lucy last night."

"Kind of sort of?" She swatted him. "Pull over or drive, but get out of the middle of the road. Either you went on a date with Lucy or you didn't."

Lane shifted into first gear. "Lucy and Carina went to dinner and I was there at the same time." He turned onto Main Street. "Carina asked me to join them and I did. How would you define it?"

When his mother didn't respond, he glanced over toward her. "I guess you kind of sort of had a dinner date with Lucy," she mumbled.

"Okay. Now that that's settled." They parked in front of The Magpie moments later. The overhead bell jingled as they walked through the door.

"As I live and breathe." Maggie Dalton, the luncheonette's owner, greeted them with a warm hug. "I don't believe my eyes. First Lucy Travisonno and now Barbara Morgan. It feels like Old Home Week around here."

"Lucy's here?" Lane scanned the handful of tables and booths in the small retro restaurant. He spotted her when Carina attempted to jump out of their booth, only to be thwarted by Lucy.

"Would y'all like to sit together?" Maggie asked.

"I don't want to intrude," Lane said.

"Nonsense." His mother quickly made her way to their booth. Lane braced himself for a potential onslaught. There was no telling what she might say to Lucy. "Aren't you a breath of fresh air?" Barbara leaned over and gave her a hug.

"Mrs. Morgan." Lucy smiled. "It's good to see you."

"How many times have I told you to call me Barbara? And this must be Carina." His mother practically hip-checked the kid to get her to scoot over. "You're as pretty as your mother." Barbara looked over her shoulder at Lane. "Don't stand there with your hat in your hands. Get yourself on over here."

Lucy and Carina were laughing—at his expense—before he reached the table. Lucy sheepishly looked up at him. "I see some things really do stay the same around here."

Lane nodded and squeezed in beside her, their hands touching briefly beneath the table. "Were you hoping I'd be here?" Lane whispered to Lucy while

Carina attempted to teach his mother a few words of Italian.

"The thought had crossed my mind." She smiled. Her hair fell freely around her shoulders, still damp from her shower. Barely any makeup and she outshone everyone else in the place.

Throughout breakfast, their legs casually brushed against each other. And they were both so apologetic that it bordered on comical. Lane wanted to reach under the table and secretly entwine his fingers with hers. It wasn't his brightest idea and was probably even the stupidest thought he'd had all week. But it drove him crazy thinking about it. He hadn't been this close to her—for this long—since they were kids.

When it came time for them to leave, his body felt heavier, as though someone had attached lead weights to his feet. He wasn't sure if it was from his country-fried steak and eggs or his reluctance to go.

After reconfirming Carina's lesson in an hour, Lane drove his mom home. It didn't take long for her to start on him. "Now I understand why you wanted to go to breakfast. You could've just told me instead of making me think you really wanted to spend time with me."

"I did, and I promise you, I didn't know she'd be there." Lane hated that his mother thought he was using her. "I genuinely want to start having our Saturday breakfasts again. And it doesn't have to be The Magpie, and it doesn't even have to be in Ramblewood. I want to spend more time with you and I usually have Saturday mornings free."

"Okay," his mother skeptically agreed. "I get to choose the place and I won't tell you where until you pick me up. But you need to promise me something."

"Anything," Lane said.

"If you give Lucy another chance—and I suspect you will—don't let her break your heart again."

Lane stopped in front of her apartment and shifted the truck into Neutral. "She has me so wound up I don't know if I'm coming or going. I never expected to see her again and now that I have, I can't imagine a world without her in it."

"Sounds like that blasted lovebug again." Barbara popped open her door. "Speaking of bugs...when you see that old codger of a bunkmate of yours, tell him he still owes me a dance after he cut out of Slater's early last week."

Lane shook his head. Rusty and his mother had been doing the dance of the non-love, non-dating, "we're just friends," "he's too old for me," "she's too young for me," non-relationship thing for a year now. "I'll call you later, Mom." He loved them both, but relationship role models they were not. Lane wanted the love, dating, "more than friends," "we're perfect for each other" relationship thing. And today more than ever, he wanted it with Lucy.

LUCY HAD CALLED Rusty after they left The Magpie and pushed their lesson back an hour. She trusted Lane with her daughter, although she wasn't sure how she could trust a man she hadn't seen in ten years. She didn't know him as an adult. She'd been back only a handful of weeks and she'd already left her child with him. Whether she trusted him or not, Lucy had made some poor choices throughout her life and she didn't want her renewed feelings for Lane to cloud her judgment when it came to her daughter's safety. This whole barrel-racing thing had her belly doing flip-flops worse than when she was on the back of a cutting horse.

Lane waited for them in front of the stables. She'd expected Carina's first lesson to be on Lane's horse. But the brown-and-cream-colored American paint by his side was much smaller than his own mount.

"Carina, this is Jigsaw." Lane ran his hand over the horse's mane. "He's the newest member of my family."

"You bought him?" Carina asked, wide-eyed.

"I did. He's much smaller than our stock and nobody else wanted him. Now you'll always have a horse to visit or ride whenever you want."

"Lane." The gesture moved and worried Lucy at the same time. "I told you we couldn't accept anything."

"And you're not. Jigsaw is my horse and I'm loaning him to your daughter." Lane flashed her an "I beat you at your own game" grin. "I've been working with him for five years, and much like with Frankie, I became too attached to let him go." Lane handed Carina the lead rope. "Would you like to walk him over to that corral on the far right?"

Carina threw her arms around Lane's waist before giving Jigsaw a hug. After they were out of earshot,

Lucy waggled a finger at him. "I think there's more to your Jigsaw story than you're telling me, but there's no replacing the smile you've put on her face. Thank you." Lane walked with her to the corral. "If you don't mind, I'm going to hang around for her lesson."

"I figured you might," Lane said.

"I'm still trying to figure out her fascination with barrel racing and complete disregard for dressage. I don't know if another kid said something to her at school or what. She won't talk to me, but maybe she will to you."

"If the opportunity presents itself, I'll see what I can find out," Lane said. "She's a perceptive kid. If I just come out and ask her, she'll know you put me up to it."

"Her drive is strong when she sets her mind to it and she can be a little difficult. I'm hanging around today because I want to make sure she listens to your instructions. She's under the impression barrel racing doesn't have many rules."

"It has plenty of rules," Lane reassured her.

"I know that you know that, but Carina's used to a very disciplined style of riding and to her, an eight-year-old-going-on-twenty know-it-all, this will be easy."

"Gotcha." Lane entered the corral with Carina and Jigsaw. "Let's start with Western Saddling 101."

Lucy sat on the fence rail, trying not to laugh. By the time Lane had Carina lift the saddle on and off Jigsaw a solid ten times, the word *easy* had faded from her vocabulary. After an hour, her daughter looked the way Lucy had after her first lesson with Rusty.

"You did good." Lane unbuckled Carina's helmet. "You have a natural ease in the saddle."

"I can't believe how different it is from English riding." Carina limped slightly as they led the horse back to the stables. "Can I groom him?"

Lucy checked her watch. She was due to meet Rusty in a few minutes.

"She can stay with me until you get back or I can drop her off at Ella's. I'm assuming you and Rusty are riding out."

Lucy nodded. Rusty felt she had advanced out of the pen and into an actual herding scenario. "I don't know how long I'll be gone." Lucy pulled her key ring from her pocket and removed her house key. "Here, in case she wants to go home. She hasn't ridden for a few months and I have a feeling she might be a little sore. She can't stay there alone, though."

"Do you have food in the house?" Lane asked.

"Of course."

"Then we'll be fine."

Lucy gnawed on her bottom lip. She didn't know why she was trusting Lane in her house with her daughter, but besides Ella and Nicolino and a few of the nannies she'd hired, she felt more secure with him around her child than anyone else.

"Go show Rusty what Italian cowgirls are made of."

Lucy gave her daughter a hug and a kiss goodbye,

then stopped herself as she almost gave one to Lane. It felt natural—like the way they should have been.

Lucy had been right. Within the hour, Carina had been ready to go home. After she'd changed out of her horse clothes and shown him around the cottage, she settled on the couch while he fixed them both a snack of sliced apples with peanut butter.

"What are we watching?" Lane sat beside her, noticing the framed photo of a man resembling Carina on the end table.

"That's my dad," Carina said, ignoring his question. "I put a picture of him in every room so he's always watching over me and Mamma. I miss him so much."

Lane swallowed hard. He knew exactly how she felt. "I know you do, munchkin."

Carina snatched an apple slice. "This is my mom's favorite snack."

Lane remembered the first time he'd made apples and peanut butter for Lucy. She'd thought it was the oddest thing until she tried it. At least she still carried some part of him with her.

"We don't get many channels. Mamma says we can't afford cable. I think cartoons are still on."

Lane flipped through the channels on the remote. "How's school? Are you making friends?"

Carina shrugged. "The cool kids are in the Junior Rodeo."

That explained her desire to switch from English to Western riding. She wanted to fit in. "Maybe we can go to a Junior Rodeo competition. But we have to run it by your mom first."

"Really? I would love that." Carina munched on her snack. "How come you don't have kids?"

She knew how to ask the hard questions. "I—I didn't think I wanted kids until recently."

"How come?" Carina asked.

It's complicated. "My dad was a truck driver. He was always on the road, so I didn't get to see much of him when I was growing up. He always promised we would spend time together later, when he could afford to take time off. Later never came. When he died, my mom worked multiple jobs to support us and I didn't get to see her much, either. I never had the chance to do kid things. I was too busy hanging around ranches learning how to be a working cowboy. I didn't want to put another kid through that."

In his mind, kids deserved parents who could not only afford them but also afford to spend time with them. It was something he noticed Lucy hadn't had the opportunity to do much of with Carina.

"You spend time with me."

Lane ruffled her hair. "I'm making more money than I was back then, and let's just say my life didn't go quite as I planned." It had veered further off course since Lucy popped back into his life.

Carina's questions had triggered a memory he'd forgotten about. He and Lucy had been planning their future together in Wyoming. A ranch hand's salary didn't pay much and they would have felt more of a crunch since Lane had planned to rent an apartment in town with her instead of living in a bunkhouse. They'd briefly discussed the possibility of a family, but they'd concluded they were too young and too poor to even consider it. At least, he thought they'd decided together. Lucy had agreed with him at the time, but maybe she hadn't meant it. He'd been so mad at her for leaving him without a word that he'd wanted to stay mad at her once he'd learned of Carina. The more time he spent around the both of them, the more he began to understand what Lucy had meant when she said if she'd never married Antonio, Carina wouldn't have existed. And he'd never wish for that. Carina was destined to be Lucy's daughter and it wouldn't have happened if she had followed him to Wyoming. He never thought he'd forgive her, but he had without even realizing it.

Carina had fallen asleep against his arm. He smiled down at her. He could get used to this. It didn't matter that she wasn't biologically his. She needed a father and for the first time in his life, he was 100 percent certain he wanted to be one.

Chapter Eight

Lucy parked next to Lane's truck in front of her cottage. It was almost three in the afternoon and she was starving. She hadn't known what to expect when she walked into the house, but she hadn't imagined what she found.

Carina and Lane had fallen asleep on the couch, her daughter against his elbow, and a half-eaten plate of brown apples and peanut butter on his lap. It appeared as though neither one of them had gotten much sleep last night. She didn't have the heart to interrupt their nap.

She set the plate in the kitchen and then ducked into the bathroom to strip out of her filthy clothes. She'd ridden horses most of her life, and yet she couldn't remember having been this dirty. After a shower, she felt human again. As hungry as she was, she didn't have the energy to eat. She eased her aching body onto the opposite end of the sofa, relishing its softness compared to the stiff, creaky saddle she'd suffered this afternoon. She'd been officially chafed in places she hadn't known she could be chafed.

She closed her eyes, enjoying Lane's rhythmic soft snores. Antonio had snored obnoxiously. She'd cursed that sound every day of their marriage. There was a mandatory two-year waiting period in Italy before a divorce. During their separation, they'd still resided together so they could coparent their daughter. She could even hear him snoring on the opposite side of the villa. When he had moved out after their divorce had been finalized, she'd found it impossible to fall asleep. She hadn't known if she'd grown accustomed to the noise or if the reality of being alone frightened her.

In a way, today had been perfect. Between breakfast with his mom and coming home to Lane and Carina, Lucy was at peace. Nothing else mattered except this moment in time. Her daughter and her first and only true love...

LANE AWOKE TO a darkened room. His neck ached and when he attempted to move, he felt extra weight on his right side. Rubbing his eyes, he tried to shake off his sleep-induced fog. When he adjusted to the dark, he remembered where he was. He gently shifted Carina off him and noticed Lucy curled up on the opposite end of the couch.

So this is what it's like. A neat little family unit, with everyone home together on the couch on a Saturday night. It had been a foreign concept to him before now. He hadn't experienced anything remotely close to this with his own family. He'd never questioned his parents' love for him or even each other, but actually feeling it had been nonexistent.

Lane debated waking Lucy, not wanting to break the spell. Lane glanced at Antonio's photo. "I promise to always do right by them," Lane said to the ceiling. "Lucy." He gently shook her awake. "I guess we were all tired."

She sat up straight on the couch, rubbing her shoulder muscles. "I think Rusty is trying to kill me."

"He's the best teacher you could ask for." Lane envisioned sitting behind her on the couch, easing the day's aches from her body. As tempted as he was, he didn't think Carina would understand the situation. Hell, he didn't even understand it.

"I'm not the greatest cook in the world, but I make an incredible chicken scampi. Carina doesn't like shrimp. You're welcome to stay for dinner." She rose and made her way to the kitchen, turning on lights along the way. "Unless you have other plans, or a date or something."

Lane joined her in the small kitchen. "I'd love to stay." He liked her this way. A pale pink T-shirt, black cropped pants, barefoot and not a stitch of makeup on her delicate features. "I don't have plans—date or otherwise."

Lucy shrugged and removed the ingredients she needed from the refrigerator.

Lane kept his voice low so he wouldn't wake Carina. "That is either the third or fourth time you've hinted about me seeing someone. Do I sense a little jealousy?"

"Hardly." Lucy feigned indifference. "I didn't want you to feel obligated to stay, that's all."

He had an unbelievable urge to tug her into his arms and reassure her with a kiss. Fearing Carina would wake up and walk in on them, he maintained a safe distance in hopes of quelling his libido. "Since we're clearing the air—"

"You're clearing the air. I'm stinking it up with onions and garlic." She wrinkled her nose and smiled.

"If we were alone," Lane whispered, "I'd brave another kiss."

Lucy's hands stilled over the cutting board. "I'd like that."

"I'm not going to ask you to go out with me alone." Lane leaned against the refrigerator, watching her facial expressions as he spoke. Her eyes fluttered closed and her breath stilled as she waited in anticipation, and he found it irresistible. "How would you feel about a trail ride tomorrow? All three of us. I'll pack a picnic lunch and we can head down to the watering hole. Maybe even go for a swim if it's warm enough."

"I want to," Lucy whispered.

"What's stopping you?"

"I'm your boss. How would it look if someone saw us together?" she asked.

"On two hundred fifty thousand acres, I think we can find a place away from prying eyes. Enough people know about our past and probably already suspect the attraction is still there." Lucy looked up at him. "It's still there, isn't it?" he asked.

She nodded and returned her attention to the cutting board. "I don't think it ever left."

"Then be with me. Spend time with me and let's see where this goes." Lucy visibly shivered. He watched the tiny goose bumps appear on her arms. "Cold?" If they'd been alone, he would have wrapped her up in his arms and held her through the night.

"Yes—no—I don't know." Lucy set down the knife. "Let's see where tomorrow leads. We don't even know how tonight is going to end. You may hate my chicken scampi and never want to see me again."

"I love Mamma's chicken scampi," Carina said from the living room.

Lucy's brows lifted. "I know you do, *mia gattina*." Gesturing toward her daughter with her chin, she continued, "She's my first priority. She's my everything."

"And rightfully so." Lane adored the way Lucy doted on her daughter. He'd always been close to his mom and could talk to her about anything, but they'd never had what he'd consider an affectionate relationship. Kids needed affection. "Does that mean we're on for tomorrow?"

"Carina," Lucy called out. "Lane wants to take us for a trail ride tomorrow. Do you want to go?"

Carina ran into the kitchen. "Can I ride Jigsaw?"

"Of course." Lane stooped to her height. "He's yours to ride whenever you'd like, as long as your mom approves."

"I can't wait." Carina danced into the living room.

"Great, she's going to be up all night again." A lone

tear trickled down her cheek. She wiped it away with her sleeve. "You're the one who's made her happy lately. Thank you."

"You don't need to thank me." Lane wanted desperately to kiss away her tears. "I'm not doing anything you wouldn't do if the situation were reversed."

With each word he spoke, Lane fell harder for the only woman who had the potential to devastate him. Two and a half weeks ago, he wouldn't have taken the risk. Today he saw that risk as a chance. A chance to regain the life they'd planned together. This time, he was holding on tight.

LUCY HAD EXPECTED to meet Lane at the stables the following morning. When he rode up to her cottage on Frankie with Jigsaw and Kentucky in tow, he won over both her and Carina. She tied her daughter for most excited.

"I didn't see any need for you to drive down to the stables." Lane dismounted and tied his horse to the hitching post near the corner of the porch. Every residence on the Bridle Dance Ranch had one or more hitching posts. The Langtrys still believed in doing things the old-fashioned way.

"I know you said I didn't have to bring anything, but I grabbed a bottle of wine, anyway." Lucy's mother had raised her never to show up empty-handed and she felt compelled to bring something—even on a trail ride. "Red okay with you?"

"Red's perfect."

Carina rode out in front of them so they could keep a close watch in case she had difficulties with Jigsaw. After a little awkwardness, Carina had a better feel for steering. Whenever Lane rode close to Lucy, he reached out for her, entwining his fingers with hers. The raw strength of his hand gently caressed hers until he temporarily broke their bond to ride alongside Carina.

Lucy didn't mind trailing behind them. She loved the way his black corduroy shirt stretched across his broad shoulders. No matter the season, Lane had always chosen to wear light straw summer cowboy hats rather than the heavier felt ones the majority of men preferred in the winter months.

By lunchtime they had reached a small Airstream trailer along Cooter Creek. They dismounted and Lane led their horses to water.

"Whose trailer is this?" Lucy secretly hoped he'd say it was his. It was located in a very secluded and beautiful section of the ranch.

"Lexi and Shane Langtry's." Lexi was Bridle Dance's equine veterinarian and Shane was one of the owners. "I asked them if we could stop here along the way. I know neither one of you is accustomed to—how should I put it—rustic bathroom facilities. The trailer has running water and electricity. Plus, I thought this would be a nice place to eat lunch."

Lucy and Carina went inside to clean up. When they returned, Lane had an elaborate meal spread across the picnic table.

"I knew what you used to like, so I relied on memory and what I've learned about Carina. I hope there's something here for everyone." Lane handed them each a paper plate. "These are roast-pork-and-sauerkraut-relish sandwiches. Over here we have Cuban sandwiches with tomato jam. I believe these are grilled brie and pear and this one is a special spicy chicken courtesy of the Ragin' Cajun."

Lucy sat down at the table in awe. She didn't even know where to begin. "You picked this all up in town?"

"Most of it's homemade. When you live in a bunkhouse with a bunch of men, you'd be surprised how many are experimental gourmet chefs. We eat really well."

Lucy couldn't believe Lane had remembered what Carina ordered at dinner the other night and had taken the time to drive into town to pick it up. "That was very thoughtful." Lucy motioned to Carina's lunch.

"I brought her water, and why don't we open the wine?" Lane removed his pocketknife from the leather case attached to his belt and flipped up the corkscrew. He laughed when Lucy handed him the bottle. "I've never seen wine like this before. 'Wild at Heart.'" He read the vintage-style label aloud. "'The minute I laid eyes on this red-blooded beauty, I knew I had to have her.'" Lane's eyes met Lucy's, and she envisioned her cheeks matching the color of the wine.

"I couldn't resist when I saw it in the store." Lucy smiled. "Call me a hopeless romantic."

Lucy sensed Lane wanted to respond but couldn't with Carina nearby. It was both a blessing and a curse.

She'd never imagined her daughter chaperoning one of her dates. Lucy enjoyed this pace. It was slow and sweet...and perfect.

LANE DIDN'T THINK the smile would ever fade from his face. He'd even had a hard time shaving this morning because of it. He'd had one of the best weekends of his life and he was sorry to see it end.

He had a surprise planned for Carina that might get him in trouble with Lucy. Even though she'd told him not to buy Carina anything, he'd decided to pick her up an early birthday gift he knew she could use. Lucy had already told him she felt the horse was too extravagant. No matter how many times he attempted to reassure her he'd had his eye on Jigsaw for a while, she didn't believe him. It was the truth.

As soon as five o'clock rolled around, he phoned Lucy and asked her and Carina to come to the tack room. When he heard them try the knob, he cracked the door and told Carina to cover her eyes. Once she was inside, he covered them for her and led her to the center of the room.

"Oh, you didn't," Lucy said. "Please tell me you didn't."

"I want to see." Carina pried at his hands.

He offered an "I'm sorry" shrug. "It's an early birthday gift."

"Let me see."

"Her birthday isn't for another month," Lucy argued.

"Hello?" Carina squirmed.

"Fine, but this is her birthday gift…for the next ten years." If Lane was blessed enough to still have them in his life ten years from now, he could live with that. Maybe. Who was he kidding? He'd spoil the kid rotten.

"I'm waiting." Carina sagged against him in surrender.

Lane removed his hands from her eyes. "It's all yours."

Carina shrieked decibels higher than he thought a human ear was capable of hearing. She ran over to the hand-tooled leather barrel-racing saddle with a pink zebra-print seat and climbed on top of it on the stand. "Is it really mine?"

"It sure is," Lane said. "That's a treeless saddle, specifically for barrel racing. Now you'll have your own saddle to train on."

"But you are still a long way from racing, Carina," Lucy reiterated. "What do you say to Lane?"

"Thank you." She climbed down and gave him a hug. "Thank you for making me one of the cool kids."

Lucy gave him a questioning gaze. He shook his head slightly. He'd share the details from his talk with Carina a little later. He glanced at the clock on the wall. "I hate to do this, but I need to get to class."

He wanted to give Lucy a hug goodbye but thought better of it. He hadn't given Carina the saddle to earn any points with her mother. He wanted to pay it forward. Despite the loss of his own father, he'd had the love and support of two additional fathers: Rusty and Curly. They had chipped in and bought him his first saddle and had even given him his first horse. Without them and horses in his life, things could have turned out very differently for him. Carina deserved that same opportunity. And he'd be honored to be there for her whenever she needed him. Sometimes family ran deeper than blood. He was living proof.

"CAN I TAKE it home and put it in my bedroom?" Carina asked after Lane left.

"No. The saddle stays in the tack room." Lane's generous gift was just that. Extremely generous and a gift unlike any she could give her daughter. Was it wrong for her to be a bit jealous of him for always being the one to make Carina happy? She knew he meant well, and she appreciated it, but she always felt as if she was letting her daughter down.

It had been the same way when Antonio was alive. He'd spoiled Carina, while Lucy had disciplined her. It had never been the other way around. And it still wasn't. Someone had to teach her daughter values and limits.

"Carina, I will let you continue to take lessons with Lane and possibly even at the rodeo school on one condition."

"I already know." Carina rolled her eyes. "I have to get good grades."

She was more intuitive than Lucy had thought, which brought her back to something else Lane had said. Somebody on the ranch would eventually tell Carina she and Lane had dated when they were teens. Lucy toyed with finding the perfect time, but no time seemed right. Especially today, when Carina was so happy. She feared once Carina told people about the gift Lane had given her, it would open a wider door of opportunity for someone to divulge information they had no business telling her daughter.

Her heart rate increased at the thought. She'd had a happy week with her kid and she wanted to keep it that way.

"I need to talk to you about something and I'm not sure how you'll react." All joy evaporated from her daughter's face. "It's nothing bad. But it is something you might overhear and have questions about."

Her daughter stood there looking up at her, blinking. Walls up once again.

"You know I came here every summer to stay with Nicolino and Ella."

Blink.

"While I was here, I had a boyfriend."

Blink. Blink.

Lucy pinched the bridge of her nose, dread creeping up her spine.

"Lane was my boyfriend for four years."

Stare. Carina didn't move a molecule. It was as if she were frozen in place.

Lucy sat down across from her on a saddle stand. She could wait it out. She could sit quietly and wonder what thoughts churned in her daughter's head. Or maybe Carina's defense mechanism was thinking of nothing and just staring. She could wait.

"Was this before you met Daddy?" Carina asked, her voice barely a whisper.

Lucy took a second to carefully formulate her answer. "I'd known your father my entire life, but we didn't begin dating until after Lane and I were over." Lucy debated how much of the story Carina needed to know and decided less was best.

"Why are you telling me this? If it was before Papà, I understand."

"Because you are spending more time with him and someone might mention it to you."

"Did you love him?"

Lucy hadn't prepared for that question. "Yes. My love for Lane was different from my love for your father. Just like my love for you is different from my love for your father."

"Okay."

"We're good?" Carina nodded, but Lucy didn't feel good about any of it. She might have told her daughter the truth, but only half of it...and half-truths were the same as lies. "If you have questions, please come ask me."

Blink.

"How would you like to take Jigsaw out for a ride?"

Carina shook her head. "I'll wait for Lane tomorrow."

At least that was a good sign. She didn't blame Lane for anything, but her demeanor had darkened from only moments ago. Lucy had taken a good day and destroyed it. Once again, her past complicated the present. It amazed her how one mistake could continue to affect lives so many years later.

"I need to close up my office before we leave.

Why don't you go check on Jigsaw? I'll meet you at his stall."

Carina left the room without a sound. Her boots didn't even make a peep.

Lucy stopped in the kitchen and snagged two carrots from the refrigerator. After she grabbed her bag, she expected to find Carina in the corridor waiting. When she didn't see her, she checked Jigsaw's stall. Carina was on the far side of the horse, hugging his neck, speaking to him in Italian. She'd confided all her secrets to animals since she could talk.

Lucy knocked on the stall door. "Do you mind if I come in? I have something Jigsaw might like."

"It's open." Carina sounded so much like her telling Ella the front door was unlocked whenever she stopped by.

Lucy handed Carina the carrots. "I know Jigsaw doesn't replace the horses you lost, but I'm confident you won't lose this one. It's okay to love him. We're not going anywhere and neither is he."

"Papà didn't think he was leaving, either," Carina said.

"Is that what you're afraid of?" Lucy asked. "That Jigsaw is going to die or leave us?"

Carina's eyes shone with wetness. "Not just Jigsaw."

"Oh, honey. Come here." Lucy wrapped her arms around her daughter. All this time, Lucy had thought Carina's greatest fear was people taking the things she loved away. She hadn't realized her daughter feared death the most.

Lucy wanted to promise her daughter Jigsaw would be okay, that she'd be okay, but she couldn't. Her daughter had learned the harsh reality that there were no guarantees in life. All they could do was hang on to the ones they loved…and never let go.

Chapter Nine

New-romance euphoria faded when you had to tell the other person they'd made a mistake. Lane had thought he was helping Lucy by doing many aspects of her job without her knowledge, but now he realized he'd been hindering her growth as a barn manager instead.

A trailer was waiting to transport six horses, and Lucy had never arranged for the Coggins reports. Every minute of delay cost the ranch money. To top it off, Cole Langtry had summoned them both to his office.

"I don't know how this happened, and honestly, I don't care." Cole paced the length of his office. "I can't have a driver waiting for us to track down Lexi to run a Coggins test, let alone six of them. We may be fortunate enough to have our own state-of-the-art on-site lab, but it doesn't do us any good if our vet is on the other side of the county. I had to send the driver away and then deal with a very irate customer. I don't like being screamed at over the phone."

"It was my fault," Lucy said. "I sent an email to Lexi about the tests yesterday, but when I checked my outbox, it was still sitting there. I knew how important this was. When I hadn't received a confirmation back from Lexi, I should have followed up on it."

Lane let out a breath of relief. At least she had remembered the tests. Her chances for survival after this meeting had increased exponentially.

Cole stopped pacing and faced Lucy. "Every day I see you trying to implement new programs and change things. While I admire your drive and dedication, I need you to focus on completing the job correctly instead."

"Yes, sir," Lucy squeaked out.

By the time Cole finished ripping them apart, half the day was gone. "We have a lot to do. I hope you don't mind working late," said Lane.

Lucy's eyes widened. "I thought you were giving Carina a lesson after work."

"I intended to." Lane hated letting anyone down, especially Carina. "I have no choice. You have no choice. As innocent as it may have been, today's mistake was huge. You're lucky it was only six horses. If they had been moving twenty or thirty for a show and that had happened, you wouldn't be here anymore."

"I get it. I screwed up. And now my daughter has to pay the price, once again." Lucy stormed away from him and then quickly doubled back. "When do I get to spend time with my kid other than my days off? Did Curly put in twelve- and fourteen-hour days?"

"He worked every day, rarely taking time off. And he was on salary, so he never took a penny more for the extra time he put in. But that was Curly. He didn't have anyone to answer to other than himself."

"So the answer is never." Lucy chewed on her bottom lip. "That's what you're telling me, right?"

"I'm not saying that." Lane knew he was screwed regardless of how he answered. His only option was to be honest. "You need to le— Once you learn the job better, the routine will come more naturally to you and it won't take as long."

"So you're telling me to give it a chance?"

"More like pick up the pace." Lane grimaced. "I know it isn't what you want to hear—"

Lucy held up her hands to stop him. "That's enough, thank you." She turned and calmly walked down the main corridor to their office and closed the door behind her. The job had hit too close to home and he knew she'd struggle to keep up with the rigorous schedule it demanded. It wasn't for lack of trying. She had great ideas. She was a hard worker and took every responsibility seriously. For the most part, she did everything correctly. But she just didn't have the speed or skill necessary to do it all. She and Nicolino needed to face the fact Lucy didn't have the experience to handle the job, and that would happen only if he stopped helping her and allowed her to stumble a few times.

Lucy sat at her desk and added to her growing double-check list. She hated that her daughter had to wait another day to try out her new saddle because of Lucy's mistake. She dialed Ella and asked if she could once again watch Carina while Lucy worked late. Of course, it was never a problem, but that didn't mean it felt right. This was a critical time in her daughter's life and Lucy was rarely there for her.

"We need to talk," Lane said, closing the door behind him.

"I'm sorry I got upset with you about Carina's lesson," Lucy began. "I don't want you to think she's some spoiled kid whose mom runs to her defense whenever she doesn't get her way. That couldn't be farther from the truth. Antonio actually accused me of the opposite on more than one occasion. I found out something last night after you left for class. She's afraid of me dying. Of Jigsaw dying and probably even you dying. That's why she's been so distant. She loved her father with all her heart and he left her."

"I suspected that and told her a little bit about my situation. I didn't get into too many specifics of what went on between my mom and dad, but I think she got the gist of it. I told her I would always be there for her to talk to if she wanted to."

"But that's the problem—she doesn't trust that you'll always be there. You could die tomorrow. So could I. All she needs to do is stand around and listen to conversations in the hallway about colic and equine influenza and West Nile. She knows it's a part of life, but she doesn't know how to deal with it. And when a psychologist tells you to take your child home because she won't talk, it's frustrating beyond words."

Lane pulled her into his arms. She needed his warmth and strength, his heartbeat pressing against hers. She allowed herself the pleasure of his gentle caress against the back of her neck. He was safe. He always had been. Here he'd given Carina and her so much after the way she'd treated him ten years ago. She didn't deserve his kindness, but she was thankful for it.

"We'll figure it out," he said against her hair. "I'll help you. I won't let you go."

Lucy looked up at him. Work be damned—she needed to feel his touch, to feel his mouth against hers. She kissed him boldly, grasping his face between her hands and bringing him closer. Her tongue urged his lips apart, eager to taste him. His hands splayed across her back, pressing her to him. She needed him, more than she'd ever needed any man.

SURPRISINGLY, CARINA HADN'T been upset about missing a lesson. She had a book report due in the morning and asked if she could work on it in Lucy and Lane's office because Ella's house was too noisy. The sun was setting on the horizon as they finished. Instead of heading home, Lane treated them to pizza in town. It wasn't Italy, but Gino's came pretty close to the real deal.

Lucy excused herself to the restroom. On the way out, she stopped and watched Lane and Carina. If she hadn't known better, she'd have thought they were father and daughter. He made her laugh. He took the time to explain things she didn't understand. He listened to her silliness. It gave her hope her daughter would accept their relationship if they chose to pursue one. The way they were heading, the possibility seemed more real each day.

It was late when they arrived home. Carina fell asleep in the car and was a bear to wake up. Lucy settled her in bed and joined Lane in the living room for a glass of wine.

"Did today feel like a hundred hours to you?" Lucy asked, rubbing her neck.

Lane sat his glass on the table and reached for her. "Let me."

Lucy glanced toward Carina's door, making sure it was still closed. She settled between his thighs, her back against his chest as his strong hands eased the knots and tension from her body. She didn't want him to stop, and if she had her way, he wouldn't. She didn't want to take the chance of Carina walking in on them, though.

"It's late," Lane said against her hair. "I should head home."

She didn't want him to go, but she knew he couldn't stay, either. She eased off the couch and walked him to the door. "Thank you for dinner tonight. And dinner on Friday. Breakfast on Saturday and lunch on Sunday." They both laughed. "The next meal is on me—I don't care how much you argue."

Lane lifted her chin with the crook of his finger and ran his thumb across her bottom lip. "You're welcome." His lips grazed hers, featherlight, gradually increasing pressure with each kiss. The slow, languid strokes of his tongue were intoxicating, more so than the wine.

"You will never take Papà's place!" Carina shouted from behind them. "I won't let you."

"Oh no." Lucy ran her hands down her face. This was what she'd been afraid of… Her daughter walking in on them together. She knew better and still chose to be irresponsible. "Lane isn't trying to replace your father. Please apologize to him."

Carina stomped into the living room like a disapproving parent.

Lane held up his hand. "Don't force her. It's okay. I understand." Lane walked past Lucy and sat down on the coffee table in front of her. "I understand how you feel right now."

Carina looked at him, tears running down her cheeks.

"When my mom started seeing someone after my dad died, I was mad, too. I thought my world had ended again. I probably asked my mom how she could betray my dad at least ten times."

"You did?" Carina swiped her eyes with the back of her arm. "What did she do?"

"She stopped seeing him. My mom always put me first, the way your mom will always put you first."

"Lane, I think it's better if we don't see each other awhile. Carina and I need time together, without anyone else." Lucy actually felt herself stop breathing. Light-headed, she needed to sit down. She didn't want to hurt her daughter, but she didn't want to lose Lane again, either. Not after starting to feel good again. Regardless of how she felt, it was the right thing to do. "Carina, when you're ready, if you're ready, then maybe we can try this again."

"I can still teach you how to ride," Lane said to Carina. "Nothing has to change between you and me." He stood and gave Carina a gentle squeeze on the shoulder. "Do you still want me to give you a lesson tomorrow?"

Carina nodded.

"Okay, then. You have your mom drop you off. It'll be all right. I'm not going anywhere," Lane said.

She wanted to walk him to the door, but Carina needed her more than he did. As the front door closed behind Lane, Lucy couldn't help feeling as if he'd been telling her goodbye. Carina's reaction had taken her by surprise. Here she was worried her daughter was substituting Lane for Antonio while her daughter felt the same way about her.

Carina turned back to her bedroom, but Lucy reached for her hand. "I want you to look at me. This walking away and not talking to me has to stop. You've hurt my feelings and you've hurt Lane's, too." Carina closed her eyes, shutting her out once again. She knew as long as she kept talking, Carina would hear her...eventually. "Nobody will ever replace your father. I won't let them. Whether it's Lane or any man. That doesn't mean there isn't room for somebody else in your life. Just because your father died doesn't mean you have to forget about him. No one's telling you to do that. I don't want you to forget him. He will always be a part of us. You need to understand that above all else."

Tears streamed down Carina's face as heavy sobs heaved from her chest. Lucy knelt before her daughter, pulling her onto her lap. Carina had cried when Antonio died, but never to this extent. She was finally letting out the pain and anger she'd fought so hard to control. It was an emotion other than anger. Other than silence.

"It's okay, *mia gattina*. I miss him, too." Lucy stroked her daughter's hair. "I'm here and I won't let you go."

Lucy was exhausted when she arrived at work the following morning. She and Carina had been up most of the night talking about Antonio. Carina wanted to know everything about her father and his family. There were even questions Lucy couldn't answer. She told Carina she didn't have to go to school today, but she had insisted. A light had reignited in her daughter. However faint, it was there.

When she entered her office, she was surprised to see Brad sitting at Lane's desk.

"Working overtime?"

He gave her a puzzled look. "I guess you haven't heard."

"Haven't heard what?" Had they fired her over the Coggins-report debacle?

Brad cocked his head to one side. "Lane and I have switched positions indefinitely."

"You've what? On whose authority? He's my employee." How could they take her assistant away without discussing it with her first? What about his night classes?

"Nicolino called me around ten last night and told me Lane was coming in to work the rest of my shift and to take his in the morning. Believe me, I'm as surprised as you are. I've been trying to get on the day shift for years."

Lucy had been right about Lane last night. He was saying goodbye…to her. She knew without even talking to Nicolino that this had been Lane's decision. And Nicolino had gone along with it. It gave Brad what he wanted and Lane what he wanted. She still should have been consulted. It affected her job the most. How much had Lane told her cousin? "Have you seen Nicolino this morning?"

"He was upstairs talking to Kenny in Human Resources. Whatever happened between you and Lane must've been huge for me to get a promotion out of the deal." Brad relaxed in the chair, and for a moment, Lucy thought he'd put his feet up on the desk. "Thank God this position pays better. I have three kids and a wife to support. We really need the money."

"I would have thought the night barn manager position paid more." Lane had even taken a pay cut to get away from her. That spoke volumes.

"Believe it or not, assistant day manager pays more." Brad stretched. "Not a lot goes on around here at night. My list of employees was a fraction of yours. This shift has more responsibility and different duties. Forgive me in advance but I'm definitely going to lean on you for help until I can figure it all out."

On top of everything, she now had to train a new assistant barn manager when she was still learning her own job. Lucy walked toward the main office. She hadn't even been sure she and Lane were together until she asked him for space. Missing him hurt… more than it had any right to.

LANE REFUSED TO ruin Lucy's relationship with her daughter. If Carina was uncomfortable with them dating, he'd give her the opportunity to warm up to him. She'd had too many changes, too quickly. He understood. The family dynamic had changed and suddenly there was another person changing it further.

A break from Lucy would do them both some good. They'd have a chance to miss each other. It was also time for Lucy to spread her wings on her own and hopefully realize the job wasn't for her. Not because he still wanted it, but because she was more interested in science and the breeding program than managing the barn. Besides, the night shift would be a welcome break… Quiet, solitude—what more did he need?

Something to do.

How could anyone enjoy this job? He'd finished his entire workload in two hours and he had ten more to go. Maybe he could take up fly tying or crossword puzzles. He wanted to call Brad and ask him what he did all night. Even with the pay cut, the position overpaid.

He made a note to call the college in the morning

to find out about transferring to day classes. He'd hate to waste a semester.

Each time he walked by Frankie to check on his handful of employees, the horse glared at him as if to say, "You're disturbing my sleep." Being alone with your thoughts was highly overrated. He'd much rather be alone with Lucy.

After a hundred push-ups, he ventured into the tack room. Damn grooms were too thorough. There wasn't one unconditioned piece of leather around. He ventured over to the employee tack. Carina's bright pink zebra-striped saddle seat stood out amid the standard brown and black leather. He didn't know if she'd show up for her next lesson. And after he'd changed shifts without discussing it with Lucy first, she might not even allow her to. He hadn't intended to hurt either one of them. He'd waited ten years to be with Lucy. He could survive a few extra weeks or months. And if Carina never wanted him to date her mother, he'd respect her decision.

Rusty's saddle looked a little worse for wear. At least that would give him something to do. At this rate, he'd never make it until the morning.

"How are you holding up, sweetie?" Ella asked.

"Fine. Carina's grades are finally improving with each test she takes. And work is…" Lucy slumped onto the couch. "Oh, Ella, it's awful. I hadn't realized how much of my job Lane had been doing until he was gone. I can't keep up. I'm supposed to be training Brad, but for the last three days I've been playing catch-up on my own work. Lane was right. Practical experience far outweighs classroom time. I was certain I could do this job, and I failed." Lucy clenched her fists. "I had to break down and call him when a feed order didn't come in."

"Is that all?" Ella laughed. "Honey, they always have a reserve on hand."

Lucy shook her head. "It was getting dangerously low. I've battled this distributor for three days and all they kept saying was that I was placing my orders too late in the day. Following that logic, the first order should have been a day late. But it never arrived. We had a bad grain shipment from another supplier come in and that had to go back. I couldn't risk depleting the reserves any further. It took hours, but Lane's contacts managed to pull in emergency deliveries from seven different suppliers to cover the next couple of days and the reserve."

"Well, see? It all worked out in the end." Ella's forced cheerleader routine looked more like a deranged rodeo clown.

"No, no. I don't deserve to be coddled." Lucy stood up and reached for her bag. "I'm finished, Ella. I questioned if I could do this job before I left Italy and I should've followed my intuition. I never should have accepted it. But I was so desperate when Nicolino called—I believed it was a sign."

"What are you going to do?" Ella asked.

Lucy removed an envelope from her bag and handed it to her.

Ella unfolded the letter tucked inside and read it.

"Nicolino won't accept your resignation without an explanation." She refolded it and set it next to them.

"I'll give him one. Heck, I'll give him twenty." Lucy checked her phone. Carina had said she'd text or call when she was finished with her riding lesson. Lane's willingness to keep his promise to Carina continued to amaze her. After her daughter's outburst the other night, she would have understood if he'd ended the lessons, too. "Nicolino needs to realize Lane's been doing the barn manager position ever since Curly left. This should have been his job. Curly had a plan in mind when he hired Lane. He may not have been able to choose his successor, but his opinion should have counted the most. Nobody knew the job better than Curly. I love my cousin dearly, but he gave the job to the wrong person. I need to spend more time with Carina. This not getting home until eight or nine o'clock isn't acceptable when you're a single parent. I'll find another job."

"Do you have anything lined up?" Ella asked. "We can float you a loan. You don't even have to ask." Ella opened the credenza drawer and withdrew her checkbook and a pen. "I'll write a check and deposit it into your account. Then you won't feel like you had to ask."

Lucy clasped Ella's hands together and gently squeezed them. "I saw an opening posted for a breeding assistant position available. I'll ask Nicolino if I can interview for it and take it from there. Either way, I'm through with barn management. Until then, please keep your money. I don't want to go to the bank and find out you've snuck money into my account. Revenge will not be pretty. I'll pay you back in stacks of pennies all over your house."

Ella's front door opened. The women stood side by side, anxiously awaiting Nicolino's arrival. It would've been more professional to meet with him in the office, but considering she rarely saw her cousin at work, his home had been her only option.

"Okay, that's not a good look. What are you two up to?" Nicolino frowned.

Lucy handed him the envelope.

"What's this?" Nicolino flipped it over in his hands and lifted the flap.

"My resignation. I quit." The words seemed more final once she'd said them aloud. "Lane has been doing my job all along. I'm a fraud and you need to hire him in my place."

Lucy recounted the days' events to Nicolino. When she'd finished, he finally agreed with her. "I accept your resignation. The job does require more experience. I hope you don't think I intentionally set you up to fail."

"A teeny part of me did, but I got over it." Lucy hugged her cousin. "I know you meant well and I appreciate the confidence you have—well, had—in me to do the job. I would appreciate another chance, though. I'd really like the breeding assistant position. I know it's entry-level, but I'm willing to take the pay cut."

"It's a significant pay cut, Lucy. That's the position I put college kids in. Not someone with your experience."

"But that's just it." Lucy had to find a way to make him understand. "I don't have any experience. Much of what I know is on paper. And even then, I have to look it up because I'm not using it on a regular basis. I've been lugging around some of my old college textbooks and my back's about to break. Lane can do the barn manager position in his sleep. He told me you worked your way up while you were in college. Why won't you grant him the same courtesy?"

"I need to sleep on it," Nicolino said.

"You say that, but you won't," Lucy challenged. "What are you so afraid of? That he'll prove you wrong? He proved me wrong and I'm still standing."

"You and Lane worked well together." Nicolino rubbed his jaw. "Would you consider working as his assistant? The salary is less than you're getting now but much more than a breeding assistant."

"No, Brad's wanted that job for years and he's thrilled with it. It wouldn't be right to bump him back to the night shift." Lucy continued, "Lane and I had just started to rediscover each other when Carina found out about us and I decided to call things off. Working together creates too much of a conflict when something goes wrong. I tried barn management, and my heart's not in it. I want to learn more about artificial insemination and broodmares."

"Okay. If you want it, then I'll run it past Lexi and Cole. If they agree, the job's yours."

"Thank you. What about Lane? Will you finally promote him?"

"Yes," Nicolino said exasperatedly. "I'll call him tonight."

Lucy cleared her throat. "Seriously? You're going to give him the promotion he busted his butt for over the phone. You're so impersonal."

"I agree," Ella said. "Don't you think you owe him more than that?"

"Fine, if it will make you two happy, I will go see him tonight and offer him the position…after I eat my dinner." Nicolino raked his fingers through his hair. "Just do me a favor. If for some reason you and Lane don't work things out, promise me you won't date another one of my employees. You wear me out."

"I promise. Lane will be my last."

Chapter Ten

"My mom's miserable without you." Carina swung a leg over Jigsaw's back.

"I'm not too happy without her, either." Besides during the food-delivery fiasco today, Lane hadn't seen or heard from Lucy. She'd always been diligent about meeting with the night manager. But now that Lane held the job, she'd officially delegated it to Brad, who was a natural fit for the assistant position.

"What are you going to do about it?" Carina said matter-of-factly, causing Lane to choke on his laughter. The dark pigtails peeking out from under her helmet reminded him of her age.

"That's up to you. I said I'd wait until you were comfortable with your mother and me spending time together." Lane adjusted the length of the stirrups on her new saddle. "How does that feel?"

She shifted slightly in the seat and nodded. "Don't you think that's a lot of responsibility to put on a kid? I'm not even nine yet and you want me to make life-changing decisions."

Above all else, he wanted her to communicate. A

lively Carina was much more fun to be around. "May I make a suggestion?"

"Mmm-hmm." Carina shortened her reins, holding them loosely in her left hand.

"How would you feel about helping me plan a special date? One that the three of us could go on together?" Lane didn't mind going on a date with Lucy and Carina. He fully understood they were a package deal, and that was what he wanted. The full package.

"I'd like that." Lane swore he could see the wheels turning in her head. "Can it be anywhere?"

"Anywhere that doesn't require airfare." He should have put limits on the location and price. Carina was used to servants, large estates and traveling the world. So was Lucy. It made him wonder if the joke was on him and he was fooling himself. How could dusty old Ramblewood possibly compete with the lavish lifestyle they'd shared with Antonio?

"She always talks about a rodeo she went to here."

Lane instantly knew which rodeo Carina meant. It was where he and Lucy had shared their first kiss. "That particular one isn't running this time of year, but there are a few others we can choose from.

"Do they have barrel racers?" Carina sat straighter in her saddle in anticipation.

Carina had Lucy's spunky enthusiasm. "The Comal County Fair and Rodeo is next weekend and I'm almost positive they'll have barrel racing."

"Do they have funnel cake and fried Snickers bars there?" Carina nudged Jigsaw forward.

Lane laughed. "They might have funnel cake, but

I'm not sure about the fried Snickers. They might have fried Oreos, though. You'll have a mighty big bellyache if you eat all that." Lane assumed the kids at school had talked about fair foods and Carina hadn't known what they were. "Why don't I look up a few things and tomorrow we'll sit down and plan our date after your lesson? But only if you're ready."

"I want Mamma to be happy." Carina's smile brightened her tiny features. "I can't wait."

Her form had improved significantly since their last lesson, presumably from her many hours spent studying the rodeo-school students from the fence rail. Hopefully, Lucy would be able to afford lessons soon. Carina would benefit from the socialization and competition. The kid thrived when she had a goal to work toward.

Lane was surprised when Nicolino arrived to pick up Carina an hour later. He'd expected to see Lucy. He hoped she understood he hadn't changed his work schedule to hurt her. He wanted to improve her relationship with Carina.

She gave Lane a hug goodbye and climbed into the backseat of the SUV while he confirmed her lessons for Saturday morning with Nicolino. Since his new hours began, he'd been able to teach her only on Friday and the weekend. He'd hoped to talk with Lucy tonight about moving her lessons from six o'clock to four, right after Carina came home from school.

"I want to apologize for not making you barn manager when Curly retired." Lane almost had a heart attack. Nicolino never apologized. His pride wouldn't allow it. "If you're still interested, it's yours."

"What happened to Lucy?" Despite his wanting the job, she'd worked hard for it. He'd had the chance to see her on one of the cutting horses earlier and she rode as if she were born in the saddle. Lane hadn't given her enough credit and now he regretted it. "She has a lot of talent—you can't just fire her over what happened today."

Nicolino held up his hand. "She didn't get fired— she resigned."

"She did what?" Lane removed his hat and slapped it against his thigh. He didn't want the position by default. "You're not giving me the job because I earned it—you're giving it to me because Lucy quit. Where is she? I need to talk some sense into her."

Nicolino leaned against the fence rail, laughing. "Man, you've got it bad for her. One of your biggest problems is how fast you jump to conclusions." Nicolino waggled his finger for emphasis. "You're quick on the draw, which won't benefit you as barn manager. For the record, Lucy decided—on her own— that she'd rather work in breed management and she's already accepted the breeding assistant position, pending approval from the department heads."

"Doesn't that job only pay a couple pennies more than minimum wage?" She had a difficult time financially already. There definitely wouldn't be any room in her new budget for Carina's riding lessons—she'd once again look like the bad guy.

Nicolino jammed his hands in his pockets. "I've

learned my lesson when it comes to Lucy. She had doubts about becoming barn manager from the beginning. I kept pushing the idea because I wanted her here. She and Carina needed stability and they needed a place to live." He kicked a stone off the path. "And I know Lucy's a hard worker. She's smart, but she's focused her education on science. I overestimated her management abilities while underestimating yours. I'm a proud man and I don't like admitting when I'm wrong, but where you and Lucy are concerned, I've made many mistakes. You'll make an excellent barn manager and I hope you accept my offer." Nicolino held out his hand.

Lane shook it. "I accept." It took a big man to apologize when he was wrong and he respected Nicolino for his honesty.

"Then I'll see you at work Monday morning. You have a good weekend." Nicolino walked toward his SUV.

"Before you go." Lane caught up with him. "Just how mad is Lucy about the whole shift-change thing?"

Nicolino laughed loudly. "She was miffed at first, but it helped her realize the job wasn't for her. I'd say you might be out of the doghouse. You two need to learn how to hash out your differences, even when they involve Carina. For a relationship to work, you have to work hard at it."

"That almost sounds like we have your blessing." Lane didn't know if he could handle the new Nicolino.

"Don't push it. I'll see you Monday and I'll do my best to convince Lucy to drop Carina off for her lesson tomorrow." Lane waved to Carina as Nicolino drove away.

He'd done it. He had the barn manager position. He'd achieved his goal and it felt empty. He wanted to celebrate. He deserved to celebrate. He'd worked his way up from mucking stalls and finally felt accomplished. Somehow it didn't mean as much without Lucy by his side.

There was only one person he wanted to share the news with, and he didn't think she'd want to celebrate a promotion that came at her expense. Whether she'd stepped down or not, she'd gone on a heck of an emotional roller-coaster ride these past few weeks. As much as he wanted to check on her, he decided it was best to stay away. She had her family to lean on. Hopefully, tomorrow they'd have a chance to talk. If not, he might have to wait until the surprise date he was planning with Carina. He'd do just about anything to make both of his cowgirls happy.

"Where are you two taking me?" Lucy wasn't a big fan of being blindfolded and driven down a bumpy country road. She had suspected Carina and Lane were up to something all week, but she hadn't anticipated a kidnapping. "Is this blindfold really necessary?"

Carina's hand squeezed hers. "Be patient, Mamma. We're almost there." She felt Carina shift on the bench seat between her and Lane. "We are almost there, right?"

"Almost," Lane said. She might not have been able

to see him, but she knew he was enjoying this as much as Carina was. "And the blindfold was your daughter's idea. She didn't want you to guess before we got there."

Lucy had been thrilled when Nicolino told her Lane had accepted the barn manager position. He was in his rightful place. And she was in hers. So what if her new job didn't pay much. Every day she looked forward to going to work. She loved interacting with the broodmares and the foals. When she assisted on an ultrasound or a delivery, she was helping to bring a new life into this world. Okay, so she wasn't an obstetrician, but with the exception of her own daughter, Lucy thought those foals were cuter than newborn babies.

"Should I be worried?" Lucy asked. "You both are too quiet." Lane and Carina laughed. "Okay, that's not very reassuring."

In spite of the blindfold, Lucy looked forward to today. Aside from when she picked Carina up from her riding lessons, which had become a daily occurrence, she rarely saw Lane at work. And when she did, it was only a brief hello in the corridor.

He'd phoned last weekend and explained his need to create distance between them. He'd also told her what Nicolino said about their relationship. She couldn't have agreed more.

As perfect as everything seemed on the outside, she'd never been more conflicted. At least when they had the job between them, she'd had a reason to stay away from Lane. It hadn't exactly stopped them, but it had given her more reason to be cautious. He was no longer her employee and her reasons for staying away were gone, except for one.

During the week, she'd made up her mind to tell Lane about the baby she'd lost. He had a right to know about the child they'd created together. It would be painful and she wasn't sure how he would handle the news or her betrayal, but she finally felt secure in her decision. She just had to find the right time, when they were truly alone without the risk of interruption.

The truck stopped.

Lucy heard the faint sound of calliope music in the distance. She lowered the window and inhaled. The heady scent of greasy street food filled the cab. Nearby, the aggressive rumble of a truck's exhaust system drowned out the sound of children playing. She smiled. She might not know where, but she knew what.

"Are we at a county fair?" Lucy asked.

"Mamma, you weren't supposed to guess." Disappointment hung on her words.

"You're half-right," Lane said. "Leave your blindfold on."

Lucy heard the driver's door creak open and Carina scoot away from her. The passenger's-side door opened, leaving her slightly unsteady since she'd been leaning against it.

Lane and Carina guided her out of the truck until she dug her boots into the soft, loose ground. "I am not taking another step with this blindfold on. Number one, I'm not coordinated enough, and number two, people will start talking."

Lane and Carina's laughter began to sound like cackling. "You two are enjoying this way too much."

Lane's muscular hands gripped her shoulders, guiding her to step forward, while he squeezed between her and the truck. The entire length of his body pressed against hers. She closed her eyes, allowing herself to enjoy the moment. Lane's hands gently untied her blindfold, allowing it to slip away.

"Surprise," his deep voice said against her cheek, almost causing her knees to buckle. Sensing her distress, Lane wrapped his arm around her waist.

"Surprise, Mamma!" Carina jumped up and down. "It's a county fair and a rodeo!"

"So this is what you two have been up to." Every time Lucy had gone to pick up Carina after her lesson, she had already been finished, off her horse and in the stables. When she'd asked why, they had repeatedly told her it was a surprise. "Carina, am I correct in assuming that this means you're okay with Lane and me?" Lucy almost hated asking the question.

"I want you to be happy, Mamma, and Lane makes you happy." Carina grabbed her hand and began pulling her toward the fair entrance.

Lane closed the truck door and quickly caught up with them. "I know this isn't the same rodeo that I took you to years ago, but this one is even better."

Lucy had expected Lane to walk next to her. She was surprised when he chose to walk on Carina's other side. When he reached for her daughter's hand,

Lucy smiled at the quaint picture they made. They should have had this life all along. Lucy refused to think of what could've been. What she had now was pretty special.

"I'm going to have funnel cake and cotton candy and a turkey leg and—"

"A bellyache," Lane interrupted. "She overheard kids in school talking about carnival food and she has it in her head to try one of everything."

"Carina, you have had funnel cake. It's like a flat *zeppole*. And I can't even begin to tell you how much turkey this girl has eaten over the years. She's had cotton candy before, too, considering it originated in Italy." Lucy ruffled Carina's hair, resulting in a mock fight. "But she was probably four or five the last time we went to a street festival. She probably doesn't even remember going."

"I've really eaten this stuff before?" Carina asked.

"See, you're not so different from the kids at school after all," Lane reassured her.

He paid for their tickets and they passed through the fairground gates. "This place is huge." Lucy tightened the grip on her daughter's hand. "Look, Carina. They have so many rides."

Carina let go of them and spun around giggling. "I want to see it all." Lucy fought back tears. She was not going to choke on their happy day. In the back of her mind, she feared once she told Lane about their baby, days like this wouldn't happen again. She refused to think about it today.

"I have a hunch this is your old Carina." Lane entwined his fingers with hers.

"Thank you." There weren't enough words to explain how grateful she was to him. "This means the world to me...to both of us."

"There's no reason to thank me." Lane lightly squeezed her hand. "I know I should have cleared a rodeo outing with you ahead of time, but she really wanted to surprise you. She said you always talk about the one I brought you to. I wonder why."

"My daughter betrayed me." She leaned into Lane, resting her head on his shoulder. "And I have no idea why I enjoyed that rodeo so much." Lucy feigned innocence.

Carina grabbed both of their hands and dragged them toward the baby barnyard area. "Look, Mamma, baby goats." She knelt on the hay and attempted to pet a tiny black-and-white pygmy goat as it jumped up, down and sideways. "I love him," Carina said.

"He's for sale." A man came over and joined them. "You can take him home today."

"Oh, no, she can't." Lucy reached for her daughter. "We don't have any room for a goat or any other animal."

"Mamma, we live on a huge ranch. We have lots of room," Carina corrected.

Lucy's face reddened at her daughter's admission. "Excuse her—we're only renting. Thank you, though." Lucy whacked Lane with her county fair map. "You could have helped me out."

"Nope." Lane shook his head, smiling. "It's all part of the experience. Every kid goes to a fair and wants to bring home an animal. And every parent—well, most, anyway—tells them no."

After petting every baby barnyard animal, wandering through the baby-chick and poultry exhibit and watching a goat show, the three of them walked down the fair's midway. Lights flashed and bells rang on impossible-to-win carnival games. Impossible until Lane won Carina a giant Tweety Bird, which he then had to carry around the fair.

"How on earth are we going to get that home?" Lucy asked as they stood in line for the Ferris wheel. "It's almost as big as she is."

"I could always tie it to the front of the truck like a hood ornament."

An empty bucket came around. Lucy and Carina sat on one side, while Lane and Tweety faced them. He draped his arm around Tweety's shoulders to help keep him in place.

"You look funny with that stuffed animal." Carina giggled as they began floating above the earth. "I thought Mamma and me were your dates."

"That was before Tweety." Lane faced the stuffed animal and gave it a peck on the cheek. "I think we make a cute couple."

"You and Mamma make the best couple." Carina smiled up at Lucy. "Are you happy now?"

Lucy pulled her daughter close and kissed the top of her head. "I couldn't be happier, *mia gattina*."

BY THE TIME seven thirty rolled around, they were ready for the rodeo. Especially Carina, who'd eaten almost the entire county fair over the course of the day, including a funnel cake and a snow cone within the past five minutes. She had butterflies painted on the sides of her face and henna tattoos from her fingertips to her elbows. And she'd placed a friendly bet with Lane on the pig races and won.

"I can't believe I have to paint her toenails for a month," he said to Lucy as they found a seat on the bleachers. He'd banished Tweety to the truck after his arm fell asleep from carrying him around.

"It could've been worse. If you won, she'd have to paint your toenails for a month," Lucy mused. "Somehow I don't think Rusty would ever let you live that one down."

Lane would have slept with his boots on if that had been the case. "You do have a point." He nudged Carina. "How are you holding up there, munchkin? You don't look green yet."

"Can I have a soft pretzel?" Her doe eyes looked up at him. She could've asked him for the moon and he would've obliged.

"Where do you put all that food?" Lane asked. "If we go and get a pretzel, we might miss the barrel racers. It about to begin."

The horizon had faded into deep shades of purple and blue, sharply contrasting the flashing neon lights of the carnival rides. The music began and horses rode onto the dirt arena, each rider carrying a different flag.

Lane leaned into Carina, explaining each flag as they rode by. She sat on the edge of her seat in anticipation as the horses lined up in a row.

"Ladies and gentlemen," the announcer boomed through the loudspeakers, "welcome to the Comal County Fair and Rodeo."

The rodeo clowns set out three evenly spaced barrels around the arena. Lane looked around at other families in the stands. For the most part, they looked happy. He wondered if that was how he appeared with Lucy and Carina. He couldn't remember ever feeling this content.

"Are you ready?" Lane said to Carina. He looked over the top of her head and winked at Lucy. Even though she was seated in the shadows of the stands, he could make out a light flush in her cheeks. Carina grabbed hold of his hand and squeezed it between both of hers. "Here we go!"

The buzzer sounded and the first competitor rode into the arena in a full run to the barrel on the far end. The horse's precise movements combined with the rider's categorical trust created unison between beauty and beast as they ran a cloverleaf pattern around three barrels. In thirteen seconds, it was over.

"Did you see that?" Carina bounced in her seat. "That was even more amazing than at the rodeo school." She turned to Lucy. "Mamma, now that you've seen it, please tell me I can barrel race."

"I never said you couldn't. I just wanted to make sure it was safe." Lucy looked to him for help. "It is safe, right? They're only out there for thirteen seconds."

"I wouldn't exactly call it a safe sport." The last thing Lane wanted to do was give Lucy a false sense of security. "It's safer than bull riding—let's look at it that way. With everything she has accomplished in dressage, I'm confident she'll be fine. She has the dedication and the drive necessary to succeed."

"Okay, once I get a little money behind me, which might take a little longer now, you can take lessons."

"About the lessons." Lane hoped he wasn't about to overstep his bounds. "When she's advanced her Western skills, the school would like to offer Carina free lessons providing she's willing to work for it."

"Work?" Lucy asked. "She's not even nine years old."

"Hear me out before you say no. I don't know how you feel about dressage right now," Lane said to Carina. "You don't have to make any decisions today, but I want you to think about something. I had a conversation with Shane Langtry, who is one of the school's owners. He was wondering if you'd like to help out the dressage instructor a few days a week after school in exchange for barrel-racing lessons."

"Would I be a teacher like Papà was?" Carina asked.

"In a way. It might be a great way for you to honor his memory. You'd help give dressage lessons to younger riders in exchange for barrel-racing lessons. They've discussed adding dressage to their roster at the school for about a year. They've had quite a few requests for it." He met Lucy's gaze. "It's something I want you to both think about."

Carina nodded. She didn't outright balk against it, so at least the possibility was there. He hoped she'd say yes, because he'd hate to see her give up such a huge part of her father that easily. The first few dressage lessons would most likely be difficult, but with his and Lucy's support, he knew she'd get through the emotional challenges. She'd learn to cherish the memories she'd shared with Antonio instead of burying them. She was a tough kid.

Lucy reached behind Carina for his hand. He knew where Carina's strength and beauty came from. Both mother and daughter were fighters and survivors and now they had a chance at being a family. *Family.* Lane couldn't believe how easily the idea popped into his head. If you had asked him three years ago, he'd probably have said no. Sure, he'd thought about it, but now that Lucy and Carina were firmly in his life, it was all he thought about.

By nine o'clock, Lane didn't think Carina would make it back to the truck. She was tired and full. He hadn't kept a running total, but he thought she'd managed to get at least one item from every food vendor. Thank God they hadn't had any fried Snickers.

Carina fell fast asleep between them before they'd even pulled out of the parking lot. He thought Lucy had fallen asleep, too, until he noticed her looking out the window. Normally, he hated riding in a vehicle with other people when no one spoke. Tonight he enjoyed it. They didn't need to talk. There was comfort in knowing his two cowgirls were right by his side. It was a feeling like no other.

The drive home from New Braunfels to Ramblewood took a little less than an hour. Lane parked the truck in front of Lucy's house. Carina woke as he turned off the ignition. He untied Tweety from the truck bed and handed the giant yellow bird to her. She thanked him and gave him a hug good-night before heading to bed.

He had every intention of leaving until Lucy asked him to stay and have a glass of wine. He'd never considered himself much of a wine drinker before Lucy. He'd always been a beer or whiskey man, but she'd changed him in many ways over the past month.

"Excuse me for one second. I want to make sure she washed all that paint off her face."

He opened a bottle of Chardonnay while he waited for her to return.

"There was no waking her. She'll probably have a butterfly-stained pillow in the morning. Oh well— that's what bleach is for. I put a wastepaper basket from the bathroom next to her bed...just in case. Thank you for today." She took the glass he handed her. "I'm glad you and Carina worked things out. You're good for her and she enjoys spending time with you."

"There is no need to explain. I enjoy spending time with her, too. She's the one who came to me saying you'd been miserable since we stopped seeing one another." Lane gave her his best Hollywood grin.

"She did what?" Lucy set her glass on the end table.

"You heard me. You couldn't live without me, so you had your daughter do your dirty work," Lane teased.

"You are so asking for it." She swung a throw pillow at him, but he surprised her by catching it and pulling her tight against his chest.

"You were saying?" He didn't wait for her to respond. His mouth crashed down upon hers—eager, seeking. He'd wanted to kiss her since the moment he picked her up. Hell, he'd wanted to kiss her since the last time they'd kissed almost two weeks ago. But he knew this was not the place to lose control. Reluctantly, he released her. "I should get going. If I stay we run the risk of that happening again."

"I hate to say good-night, but I'm as exhausted as she is." Lucy walked him to the door. "Thank you again for a wonderful evening. I hope this is the beginning of many more to come."

Lane summoned the restraint to give her only a quick peck goodbye. He would have preferred to spend the night making love to her, but they definitely weren't there yet. They had time. They had a future, and most of all, they had each other.

Chapter Eleven

Despite working in the same building, Lane rarely saw Lucy during business hours, which was probably for the best. He had an increasingly difficult time not kissing her whenever he did. She'd been spending more time in the ranch's state-of-the-art lab and less time in the stables. She loved her job and Cole had already given her a promotion.

After a month of lessons, Carina had progressed to the point where Lane couldn't teach her any more. Not because he didn't want to, but because she needed a barrel-racing instructor who could take her to the next level. This afternoon he planned to tell her it was time to move on. He'd tried repeatedly over the past week, but she wouldn't have any of it. He'd decided that today—Friday—would be her last lesson. As much as he'd miss their time together every afternoon, he knew he was sending her into good hands. He didn't know who it would be harder on today, her or him.

Carina was already leading Jigsaw out of his stall when he arrived.

"How was school today?" Lane gave her a hug hello.

"I got an A on my science exam and an A-plus on Texas history." Carina beamed with pride.

"Excellent!" Lane couldn't have been prouder of her if she'd been his own daughter. "That's two As. You know what that means, Jigsaw?"

"I do, I do." Carina excitedly bounced. "He gets two carrots."

"He sure does." Lane had come up with the idea of Jigsaw Treats for As on the drive home from the county fair two weeks ago. It had given Carina extra incentive to work harder in school. For all intents and purposes, Jigsaw was her horse. He'd just let Lucy believe otherwise. Speaking of Lucy, he wanted her to know he was definitely telling Carina today. "Saddle up Jigsaw, and I will meet you out there. I have to take care of something first. I'll bring the carrots when I come back."

Lane turned down the breeding corridor. He'd affectionately nicknamed it Lucy's World after she'd accepted the breeding assistant position. As he reached for the door, it opened.

"Oh my God, Lane," Lexi said. "You scared me half to death. Are you looking for Lucy?"

He nodded. "Is she in?"

"Sure, go ahead."

He waited to speak until the door completely closed behind him. Lucy was too engrossed in a microscope to notice he was there. She looked different than she had the first day she'd arrived. She'd appeared more regal and rigid back then. Six weeks later, she was more relaxed—more country. Her hair was pulled high on her head in a luxuriously full ponytail. Her faded buttery-soft boot-cut jeans, bedazzled red plaid shirt and cowboy boots were a million miles away from her English riding boots and breeches. Since her new job afforded her more time off, Lucy, Ella and the kids had made numerous trips to secondhand stores for clothes they could repurpose. His Italian cowgirl was all Texas now. If it hadn't been for her long white lab coat, he'd have thought she was ready for a night out dancing at Slater's Mill.

He cleared his throat. "Lucy."

Her body visibly quivered at the sound of his voice. He might not be able to see them right now, but he suspected he had just given her a good case of goose bumps.

"One second," she said without looking up from her microscope. "I just need to check one thing."

"I don't want to keep you from anything. I just wanted to tell you about Carina."

Her head popped up. "Is she okay?"

Lane immediately wished she had kept her attention on the microscope. Her intoxicating hazel eyes dulled his senses every time he looked into them. "She's fine. Right now. She might not be in a couple hours."

"So you are going to tell her today?" Lucy frowned. "She still hasn't said anything to me about it, but she senses it's coming. Her reluctance to talk about it makes me think she believes it will affect our relationship."

"I think so, too. I'll reassure her the best I can," Lane said. "She's advanced at an incredible rate, which I expected with her background. I'm holding her back when she deserves to fly. There's just nothing left for me to teach her unless you want her on the back of a cutting horse."

"Don't you dare." Lucy sighed. "I'll be consoling both of you tonight, won't I?"

"Why didn't you warn me kids could break your heart?" Lane teased. "I don't know who this is going to be harder on, her or me. Is it all right if I tell her she can take Jigsaw out whenever she wants? Or that she can ride with me whenever she wants? Of course, you're welcome to take Frankie out with her."

"Yeah, that's fine." Lucy wrinkled her brow. "Come over for dinner tonight and we'll plan to do something tomorrow so she understands nothing else is changing. I did speak to the rodeo school today about their future dressage plans, and it's still a work in progress. They hope to have something together by the first of the year and then she'll be able to help with the students. She'll have to wait until then."

Lane wondered if that was the real reason Carina hadn't wanted to stop their lessons. It would mean no lessons for a couple months. "I know you're going to give me an argument about this, but I'm going to do it, anyway. I will pay for her lessons until they implement the program. And if you're that uncomfortable with it, then call it a loan and pay me back sometime over the next fifty years. I want to see how far she can go. Not just with barrel racing, but also with dressage and possibly even Western dressage. She has so much ahead of her."

Lucy exhaled. "I'm not going to argue with you. I know how much this means to you. Probably as much as it does to her."

"Then it's settled, then. I'll see what I can do to get her into Monday's class. I can't make any guarantees, though." Lane turned and opened the door. "Wish me luck."

"Good luck," she called out to him. "Don't forget about dinner later."

"I won't." He waved to her over his head.

On the way to the round pen, he stopped in the kitchen and grabbed two carrots. Outside, Carina was trotting Jigsaw around the pen. The late-October air carried a slight chill. He stood at the fence and waited for her to ride over. But she didn't. She kept her distance and stayed on the far end of the pen. She knew and she was doing her best to avoid conversation. After watching her ride for a half hour, he decided to rip the bandage off. She clearly wasn't in the mood for a lesson, and he'd rather remember yesterday as her last lesson.

She continued to circle him in the pen until he waved a carrot. Jigsaw had zero self-control when it came to his favorite orange treat. As hard as Carina tried to stop him, the horse was coming straight to Lane.

"Carina, I know what you're doing."

"And I know what you're trying to do," she countered.

Lane reached for Jigsaw's halter before she could turn him away. "Don't you want to fly with the big girls? It's all you've talked about."

"I want to fly with you." Carina's piercing hazel eyes held his.

"This isn't all we have." Lane hated to see her fear of abandonment prevent her from moving forward in life, whether it be with him or anyone. "I'm not leaving you. I'll still be right here. You can see me every day if you want. You'll be in class while I'm still at work, and if you want to meet afterward, we can. Just text me when and where, and I'll be there. You're still going to see me on weekends."

"Mamma said she couldn't afford the rodeo school right now." Carina pouted. "Without you I'll have nothing."

"Your rodeo school is being taken care of and you might be able to start on Monday." Lane covered her hands with his. "Will you do this for me? Will you show me how far you can take these classes?"

Carina nodded. "Will you ride with me?"

"I'll ride with you whenever you want."

"Ride with me now?" she asked. "Instead of a lesson."

"You stay here while I saddle Frankie, okay?" Lane couldn't remember another child who'd affected him the way Carina had. There wasn't anything he wouldn't do for her or Lucy. And if their relationship kept progressing the way it was, he planned to propose to Lucy on Christmas.

LANE AND CARINA had been on one of the ranch trails for the past hour. She talked to him about everything from class to boys. He hadn't been prepared for the boy talk.

"Can I use Jigsaw for my barrel-racing lessons?"

"I'm afraid not. Jigsaw was bred to be a cutting horse, so he has a natural ability to cut cattle, but he's definitely a Western pleasure horse. Barrel horses have been specially trained, just like cutters." The sun had already dipped beyond the horizon and neither one of them was equipped for riding in the dark tonight. "We need to head back. We need to meet your mom for dinner."

"How fast can Jigsaw run?" Carina asked.

Why did kids always ask that question about the horses they rode? "Jigsaw's never run full out with a rider."

"I'll race you back home." Carina stood slightly in her stirrups and gripped the reins tight.

"What are you doing?" The hair stood up on the back of his neck. "This isn't the Kentucky Derby and we're not going to race these horses." And that was when he saw it. The mischievous twinkle her mother had when she was a teenager. "Carina, promise me."

Carina lowered herself back in the saddle. "You're no fun." She playfully pouted.

"Now I'm insulted," Lane teased. He rubbed the back of his neck, still sensing something wasn't right.

He took stock of her seat position and posture. She was relaxed, not ready to run. But something felt off. "Carina, ride closer to me."

"What's wrong?" she asked, glancing around them.

"I don't know. Just a gut feeling." Lane squinted in a vain attempt to see farther in the distance. Increasing cloud cover darkened the sky, hiding the sliver of a moon. "Keep your eyes open. Stay sharp and alert."

He reached for his two-way radio and remembered he'd left it on his desk. It wasn't uncommon to spot a bobcat or two on the ranch. As long as they kept their distance, they would be fine. He shifted slightly in the saddle and took out his cell phone. He was pulling Shane's number up on the screen when a slight vibrating sound caught his attention. Before he realized what it was, it struck.

Jigsaw squealed, rearing up on his hind legs. Carina screamed as she struggled to hang on. The horse began to buck wildly and then took off in a full gallop. Lane spurred Frankie after her. He needed to keep her in sight. It was too dark and they were too far out from the ranch.

"Carina!" Her silhouette faded into the night, leaving him to follow the sound of her screams.

And then they stopped.

He couldn't hear her any longer. "Carina! Carina!" He reined Frankie to a stop and listened.

Nothing. Where were they?

"Carina!"

If she had fallen off Jigsaw, he feared he'd trample her in the darkness. If she'd gotten hung up in the saddle and the horse was dragging her, he feared he'd be too late.

"Carina!"

He nudged Frankie into a trot, allowing him to see small sections of the ground in front of them when the clouds briefly parted.

"Carina!"

He searched frantically. He reached back into his pocket for his phone, only to discover he had dropped it when Jigsaw reared. He stopped once again and listened.

"Carina!"

"Lane!" It was faint, but he heard it.

"Carina!" he shouted. "Keep calling my name until I reach you!"

Up ahead in the distance, he saw the flash of a tiny white light. He guided Frankie toward it. It was Carina; it had to be her. As he approached, he slowed the horse down, unable to judge how far away he was from the light. It seemed so tiny, so remote, and then he realized what it was. It was a flashlight on Carina's phone.

He jumped off his mount and ran to her, then fell to his knees beside her.

"Lane," she cried. "Lane, help me!"

Lane took the phone from her hand and scanned her body with the light. Cuts and scratches covered her hands and face. "I'm here, baby, I'm here. Tell me where it hurts."

Carina tried to sit up, screaming from the pain. "My shoulder!"

He held the flashlight above her and pulled away her shirt. It was definitely dislocated, if not broken.

"Tell me if anything hurts." He ran his hands down both of her legs, across her arms and her rib cage. She attempted to sit again, rolling onto her right side first. "Carina, lie still. I'm calling for help."

She fought against him to get on her knees. "We need to find Jigsaw. He's hurt."

"So are you." Lane quickly dialed Shane's number on Carina's phone.

"Hello!" Shane's voice boomed through the phone.

"I'm with Carina and she's hurt." He switched the phone to speaker and set it on the ground.

"Lane! Where are you? Are you okay? I heard screaming when you called me. We're tracking your phone now."

Lane didn't even remember pressing the button to connect the call, but thankfully he had. They were looking for them.

"I lost my phone and Jigsaw. It was a rattlesnake strike. Frankie's with me. I need to get Carina to the hospital." He looked up at the stars to establish his direction, but the sky was too overcast. *Dammit!* "We took the Northwoods Trail. We were heading back to the ranch when I lost my phone. I think we're southwest of the trail, but I'm not sure. I lost all sense of direction when I was chasing after Carina."

"We're on the way," Shane said. "I have five vehicles out. We'll find you.

"We need to get Jigsaw." Carina shifted. "My shoulder and my head hurt."

If they hadn't ventured off the trail, they could have ridden back to the stables. He was so twisted around after chasing Jigsaw that he didn't want to take the chance. Lane had no idea how much time had passed when he heard an engine roaring in the distance.

"Shane." Lane picked up the phone. "I hear a vehicle. Someone's close. I see headlights!"

He turned Carina's phone around and waved the flashlight back and forth in the air.

"Over here! We're over here!" Shane's black Jeep pulled alongside them. "We need to get her to the hospital," said Lane.

Lexi jumped out of the passenger side and ran to Carina. She flipped open a first-aid kit and began to check the child's injuries. "It appears to only be her shoulder, but I don't like the looks of it. Let's get her out of here."

"You drive," Shane said to Lexi. "I'll take Frankie and see if I can find Jigsaw."

Lane lifted Carina into his arms. "Call Lucy and tell her to meet us there."

If anything happened to Carina, he'd never forgive himself. She was his responsibility and he'd stupidly taken her on a trail too close to sunset. He'd be surprised if Lucy ever spoke to him again.

Once she was tucked safely in the backseat of the Jeep, he held Carina in his arms. "It's going be okay. I won't leave you." He kissed the top of her head as she sobbed softly against his chest. He didn't know if it was from the pain, the fright or both.

"Will Jigsaw die?" she asked.

"Shane is out looking for him." He met Lexi's eyes in the rearview mirror.

"Hey, sweetie," Lexi said from the front seat. "It sounds to me like Jigsaw was bitten on the leg. He's healthy and in great shape. We may have some tissue damage to deal with, but we'll know more when we find him. As soon as they find him, I will go treat him. Okay?"

"It was all my fault," Carina said. "I wanted to go fast. I should be more careful what I wish for."

Lane laughed quietly against her hair. She'd been thrown from a horse and had done heaven-knows-what to her shoulder and she still found humor in the situation. Forget waiting until Christmas to propose. He loved them both too much. If Lucy would still talk to him after tonight, he wanted to officially make them a family.

LUCY COULDN'T GET to the hospital fast enough. Shane had said nothing looked life threatening, but after Antonio had died in a matter of minutes, she didn't trust that diagnosis. She forced herself to drive the speed limit, lest she wind up in a hospital bed alongside her daughter. After circling the hospital's parking lot, she finally found the emergency-room entrance.

"My daughter." Lucy ran to the desk. "I need to see my daughter, Carina—"

"Lucy," Lexi called out to her from the hallway behind the desk. "She's in here."

She started to walk around the desk when she caught a glimpse of Lane standing in the waiting area.

"What the hell were you thinking?" Lucy stormed over to him. "You took my child on a trail ride, in the dark, without even telling me. You don't do that. You always tell a parent where you're taking their child."

"You're right," Lane said. "I had just finished telling Carina about the rodeo school—"

"She can forget about that." Dressage was tame and methodic compared to all this Wild West chasing around. "It's too dangerous. I don't need my daughter racing forty miles per hour around a barrel. That's insane and I never should have allowed you to fill her head with these crazy ideas."

"I didn't fill her head with anything," Lane argued. "The last time I checked, you work next to a rodeo school. Carina was interested in those horses long before she knew who I was. She wasn't barrel racing when she got hurt. A rattlesnake bit Jigsaw. And if they don't find him, or if they find him and it's too late, it will be one more disappointment in her life."

After she'd lost all of their horses in Italy, Lucy didn't know how Carina would react if something happened to Jigsaw.

"Why aren't you out there looking for him?" It was his horse, his responsibility.

"Shane and some of the ranch hands are out there looking on ATVs and horseback," Lane said. "I'm not leaving here until I know Carina is okay. You both mean everything to me."

Lucy took a step toward him. She wanted yell at,

slap and hug him all at the same time. Carina was her world. "I realize this was an accident, Lane. I do. I—I need to see my daughter."

She made her way down a short hallway to a small private room.

"Oh my—" Lucy wasn't prepared to see numerous cuts on her child. When Shane had said she'd injured her shoulder, that was all she'd pictured. "My poor baby."

She held her daughter's bruised hand in hers. The last time she'd seen Carina in the hospital, she'd been in an incubator, connected to machines.

"Lucy, it looks worse than it is," Lexi said. "Everything is superficial, except for her shoulder. They brought her back from radiology no more than ten minutes ago. They believe she separated her shoulder, but we'll know shortly."

"Is Lane outside?" Carina asked.

"Honey, you need to rest." Lucy pulled a handful of paper towels from the dispenser and ran them under warm water. She held her daughter's arm and gently began to wash away a spot of dirt and blood the nurse had missed.

"Lane told me he wouldn't leave me. I need to know. They wouldn't let him in."

"They wouldn't?"

"He's not a family member, so they told him he had to wait outside," Lexi said.

"How were you able to stay with her, then?"

Lexi smiled. "I'm married to a Langtry. Nicolino is married to a Slater. And the Langtrys and Slaters own Bridle Dance. So in a roundabout way, I'm a family member. It was either that or she'd have to stay in here alone."

"I appreciate your help." Lucy continued wiping Carina's arms and face. "Thank you for taking care of her and getting her here."

"Don't thank me—thank Lane. He's the one who found her. He's your hero."

"Found her? I thought they were together." Lucy forced herself to calm down. She needed to hear the entire story.

"We were," Carina said. "Then a snake bit Jigsaw and made him take off. I held on as long as I could and then I fell. Lane had to search the ranch for me in the dark. But I turned on the flashlight on my phone and that's how he found me. Don't be mad at Lane, Mamma."

Lucy had no idea her daughter had been through such an ordeal. All Shane had told her was that they had been on a trail in the dark and Carina had fallen. She hadn't known her daughter had been missing.

Lexi's phone buzzed across her chair. Picking it up, she smiled. "That was a text about Jigsaw. They've found him and they're trailering him back to the stables. I'm going to head there and give him a thorough exam."

"Why can't he walk home?" Carina asked.

"Because the venom will spread quicker. Although after all the running he's done, it probably wouldn't have mattered much. One of my techs is with him and says he looks good." She gave Carina a kiss goodbye on the forehead. "I'll give you a full report later."

"You'll tell Lane about Jigsaw on your way out?" Lucy whispered to Lexi.

Lexi gave her arm a reassuring squeeze. "Keep me updated on Carina."

A few minutes later the door opened. "Hello, I'm Dr. Sheila Lindstrom and this is Nurse Mariah. I hear you had quite an adventure. You can call me Doc, Sheila, Linny, whatever you'd like." She crossed the room to the light box hanging on the wall and flipped it on. "I have your films." She held the first one up to the light and clipped it on the box. "I don't see any chips, breaks, fractures or dislocations." She repeated the process on the next three. "Everything looks great. You do have a separated shoulder, so I don't want you doing any riding for at least a month." Dr. Lindstrom turned to Lucy. "You'll need to follow up with her doctor after then." Sheila looked down at Carina. "You'll need to wear a sling awhile but we'll find you a really pretty one." She turned her attention to the nurse. "I want these wounds on her face and arms flushed." She rested her hand on Carina's arm. "Then we'll bandage you up and send you home."

"Thank you, Dr. Lindstrom," Lucy said. "Will you be okay in here with the nurse for a few minutes while I tell Lane what the doctor said?"

"Mamma, after today I can handle anything."

"I'm sure you can, but let's not find out, okay? I'll be back shortly."

She's going to be all right. Lucy stepped into the

hallway and flattened her back against the wall. If the doctor's report had been anything more serious, she didn't know what she would've done.

Lucy found Lane exactly where she'd left him standing in the waiting area. Lines of concern were etched on his features.

"I owe you an apology." Lucy tucked herself against his chest, allowing his arms to cocoon her in safety. On some levels, an apology didn't seem like enough after the way she'd yelled at him. "I didn't know the whole story. Lexi and Carina filled me in and I am so grateful to you. I shouldn't have spoken to you that way."

"Apology accepted." Lane gave her a half smile. "How is she?"

"It's a separated shoulder. She'll have to wear a sling for a while. Outside of some cuts and scrapes, she'll be fine."

"I really am sorry," Lane whispered against her hair. "I lost track of time."

Lucy withdrew from his arms and looked up at him. "Accidents happen when you have children. Unfortunately. She's fallen off a horse more times than I can count. I overreacted. I know how much you love Carina and you'd never put her life in jeopardy."

Lane took her hands in his. "She's not the only one I love."

Chapter Twelve

Lane had told her he loved her and Lucy hadn't said it back. She wanted to, but she couldn't...at least not yet. Between Carina's accident and still needing to tell him about their son, the timing hadn't been right.

Lane pulled her car in front of her cottage and hopped out. He hadn't had a way home from the hospital and offered to drive her car so she could ride in the back with her daughter. The pain meds the doctor had given Carina had knocked her out. Lane opened the door and gingerly lifted her out of Lucy's arms. He followed her up the porch stairs and waited for her to unlock the door.

After he laid Carina on top of her bedcovers, Lucy followed him into the living room.

"I think we could both use a glass of wine." She held her soiled shirt away from her body. "How did you manage to stay clean?"

"These are Shane's." Lane glanced down at the track pants and T-shirt he was wearing. "I don't know how clean they are but they were cleaner than what I had on. Lexi told me to take them." He patted the pants. "Actually, she has my wallet and my keys, too. That's not good. And I lost my phone. Can I borrow yours so I can call her?"

"Go ahead." Lucy removed her cell phone from her bag and handed it to him. "I'm going to clean up and get her in some clean clothes. Will you still be here when I get back? Because we really need to talk."

"I'm not going anywhere."

After Lucy wrangled Carina's dirty clothes off her and tucked her into bed, she breathed a sigh of relief. Her daughter was home. Safe. She kissed her forehead and slipped back out the door.

She grabbed a T-shirt and yoga pants from her drawer, then padded into the bathroom and stripped out of her shirt. She unbuttoned her jeans, lowered the zipper and hooked her thumbs into the waistband just as the door opened.

"I am so sorry. I thought you were in the bedroom." Lucy quickly reached for her shirt. As Lane turned to exit, he caught her reflection in the full-length mirror. He stopped and faced her. "Is that my name?"

Lucy swallowed hard. She had planned to tell him this evening, but she'd thought she'd have a few more minutes to prepare. *Prepare what?* No amount of preparation would cushion this blow.

Lane entered the bathroom and closed the door behind him, his expression blank—she couldn't read any emotion. "May I see it?" he asked, his voice throaty and low.

Lucy clutched her shirt tighter to her breasts. She

didn't know how to do this. She didn't know how to tell him it wasn't his name. She crossed the room and turned sideways. She slowly raised her arm, exposing the tattoo that ran along her rib cage, slightly above the bra line. She'd managed to keep it hidden from everyone for ten years, except Antonio, who'd been with her when she'd gotten it.

Lane reached out to touch it and then hesitated. She nodded to him that it was okay. She couldn't keep lying to him; he needed to know the truth. He deserved to know the truth. Now.

His rough fingers lightly grazed her tattoo. One word, written in delicate script, almost the length of her palm... Lane.

"I don't understand." His eyes shone. "If you felt this strongly, then why did you leave me? Why did you marry someone else and have his baby? Why is my name tattooed on your body?"

Lucy stepped away from him, slipping her shirt back over her head. If she didn't say it now, she never would. "It's not your name."

"What do you mean, it's not my name?" He laughed nervously. "How many Lanes do you know?"

She held up two fingers, willing herself to tell him the truth.

"Come on, Lucy. You don't expect me to believe that you fell in love with two men named Lane and then had the other man's name tattooed on your body. What's going on?"

She took a deep breath and exhaled slowly, holding on to the sink for support. "Lane was our son."

He swayed unsteadily. "O-Our son?" Lane looked around the bathroom. "I need to sit down." He shoved the shower curtain aside and sat on the edge of the tub. "I—we—we have a son?" Lane raked his hands through his hair. "And here I felt guilty for asking if Carina was my daughter." He attempted to smile, stood, then quickly sat back down. "Where? Where is my son? You named him Lane?" A proud grin spread across his face. "He's with your parents, right? It makes sense now. This is why you never came back? Answer me, Lucy," Lane pleaded.

She knelt on the floor in front of him, taking his hands in hers. "I never wanted to have to tell you this."

"Don't." Lane stood and flattened his back against the door. "Don't you dare tell me you gave our son up for adoption. You couldn't have. You—you wouldn't have, right?"

Lucy stayed where she was on the floor. "Our son didn't make it."

"No." Lane slid down the wall. "What are you saying?" Tears trailed down his cheeks.

"When I left here that final summer, I fully intended on coming back the following year and living in Wyoming with you. When I got home, I found out I was two months pregnant." Lucy's throat was so dry she found it almost impossible to swallow. She opened her mouth and the words wouldn't come. She reached for the sink, pulled herself up and turned the faucet on. She cupped her hand for a drink and then splashed water on her face.

I don't know how to do this.

She lowered herself onto the edge of the tub, while he remained on the floor. "I miscarried four months into the pregnancy."

He shifted to face her, taking her hands in his. "Oh, Lucy. I am so sorry. Why didn't you tell me? I would've come to you."

"I didn't tell you I was pregnant, because you didn't want kids. You were pretty adamant about it back then. You made sure we were well protected every time."

"We couldn't afford a child, Lucy. We were teenagers," Lane reasoned. "We talked about it. But that doesn't mean I wouldn't have welcomed a child if one had come along. Clearly no birth control's 100 percent. So that's why you didn't tell me. Because I said we couldn't afford kids?"

"It's more than that."

"Even if you didn't want to tell me, I don't understand why you didn't come back the following year. It doesn't make sense to me. You married Antonio while I was waiting for you. You had his child. Who was he to you?"

Lucy rubbed her forehead. He might have understood everything to this point but he wouldn't understand what she'd say next. "I had just turned eighteen, I still had one more year of school to go, I was pregnant and I didn't know what to do. You said no children—we said no children—and I didn't think I wanted children until I was actually faced with it."

"I get that. Why didn't you consider that maybe I

would've felt that way, too? Why didn't you allow me the same courtesy you gave yourself?"

Lucy silently prayed for strength. "You had started a new job in Wyoming and barely had enough money for yourself. You couldn't have afforded a baby and me. I had to make a decision and giving up our child was not an option."

"Wait a minute." Lane held up his hands. "Are you telling me you married Antonio when you knew you were carrying my baby? Tell me that's not true." Lane rose from the bathroom floor, towering above her. "What did you do, sleep with him and tell him the baby was his?"

Lucy stared at her feet. "No. I would never do that. Antonio knew the baby was yours. My parents urged me to marry him. I had known him my entire life. He was a great man and he wanted to protect me. We married right away so everyone would think the baby was his. I was under a lot of stress, between the pregnancy and morning sickness, my parents, and school. The doctors had warned me my blood pressure was too high. My pregnancy wasn't high risk yet, but it was close to it. And then one night it was all over."

Lane sat next to her on the tub. "What happened?"

"I woke up with cramps, Antonio rushed me to the hospital and by then it was too late. He was already gone." Every tear Lucy had fought back for the past month finally let loose. "When they told me it was a boy, they asked me if I wanted to name him. The only name I ever wanted to name our son was Lane."

"And your husband didn't mind?" Lane's voice was thick with doubt.

"No. Antonio wasn't like that. He was the kind of man you would have respected. He married me to save my reputation and my family's. Italy is very different from here, especially the small village where I lived. Antonio was a very wealthy man and promised to provide for our child."

"Who does that?" Lane stood and paced the tiny room in two steps. "What man takes on another man's child and willingly raises it as his own?"

"You." Lucy got to her feet. "Don't you see? You did the same thing. I know you love Carina. I know you love me. You were willing to take on Antonio's child as if she was your own. The circumstances are different, but it's still the same thing." She reached out for him but he flinched at her touch. "You never judged Carina for having a different father or held it against her. You and Antonio were very different, but you were alike in many ways. I see that now—I wish I had seen it then. You don't know how many times I've asked myself if our child would've survived if I had told you and we had tried to work through it together, but I felt unburdening myself would've been selfish. You can't change the past. I lost our child. Me. It's all on me. A day doesn't go by that I don't think about the undue stress that I put our baby through. I paid the price for my lies. So did our son. That doesn't go away and it doesn't get any better. Ella told me—"

"Ella and Nicolino knew?" Lane laughed. "Of course they did. That explains it. After ten years,

I finally know why your cousin has a problem with me. It's because I got you pregnant. They could have told me."

"It wasn't their place to tell you I was pregnant, especially when I told them not to. I asked Nicolino to tell you I wasn't coming back, but he feared you'd ask too many questions, so he chose to say nothing."

"He was right, I would have." Lane swung open the bathroom door. "I need to get out of here."

"You don't understand." Lucy followed him, her voice low so as not to wake Carina. "This wasn't easy for me."

"Well, I guess I'll never know, because you didn't trust me enough to tell me." Lane reached for the doorknob and then spun to face her. "I thought of a million reasons why you left me the way you did, but this never entered my mind. You and I—wow, Lucy. You and I could have had it all. All you had to do was tell me the truth."

Lucy smirked. "I knew you'd blame me for the miscarriage."

"I'm not blaming you for the miscarriage." Lane gripped both of her shoulders and lowered his head to hers. "I think *you've* spent the last ten years blaming yourself for the miscarriage, but just so we don't have any misunderstandings, I don't blame you for that. Miscarriages happen for all sorts of reasons. You need to let that go and forgive yourself." He released her and stepped backward, creating more distance between them.

"Then what did you mean, we could have had it all?" Lucy asked.

"Honestly, I don't know." Lane grabbed one of the kitchen bar stools and sat down. "I actually thought about this a few weeks ago. I felt you and I were meant to break up ten years ago so you could marry Antonio and have Carina. I'm not going to cheapen her existence by saying you should have told me about the pregnancy and moved to Wyoming and our son may or may not have been born. To do that would eliminate her life and I would never wish her away. So I can't answer you. All the scenarios hurt. But what hurts the most is the fact that you married another man while carrying my baby and consciously planned to pass him off as your husband's child. I can't forgive that. I'm sorry, Lucy. I love you and always will, but I have my limits."

Lucy had expected as much. Well, she'd expected less. Another declaration of love only fanned the flames higher. "What about Carina? I need to know what to tell her."

"I hold nothing against your daughter. I will continue to be there for her whenever she needs me." Lane stood and crossed the room to the front door. "She can call, visit, go riding—well, after tonight she'll need a break from that—but I'm here for her. And I'll probably even be there for you, too… someday. You need to give me some space."

"How do I explain this to my daughter? She believes we're a couple."

"Don't do that, Lucy." Lane reached for the doorknob again. "Don't you make me feel like the bad guy. You married another man while you were pregnant with my baby. Were you ever planning to tell me? If I hadn't walked in on you changing, would you have told me?"

"Yes. I was planning to tonight. That's why I didn't tell you I loved you at the hospital. Love means no secrets. No lies. I couldn't say *I love you* with a clear conscience."

A pair of headlights filtered in through the front windows. "That's Lexi." He opened the door and motioned for Lexi to give him a minute. "I need to go."

Lucy walked away from the front door and gripped the edges of the kitchen counter. "Fine. You know the truth now. So just go."

She waited for the front door to close. Every second that ticked by felt like an eternity. She didn't want to turn around and face him. She heard the door click and the floor creak behind her. His arms encircled her waist as she sagged against him.

"I'm sorry you felt you couldn't tell me," he said against her hair. "And I'm sorry that he's gone. I can't even begin to imagine what you've been through."

Lucy turned in his arms and took his face in her hands. "You need to believe me—I loved our child. He was loved."

Lane wrapped her in his arms. "I know you did. I know."

"Thank you. You don't know how much that means to me." Lucy finally allowed herself to relax in his arms. Every kiss, every touch they'd shared had so much anxiety behind it and now she was free. "You're still leaving me, aren't you?"

Lane kissed the top of her head. "We need some space from one another and I need a chance to absorb all of this. I don't know how to forgive you and until I do, I can't be with you. I can't tell you how long that feeling is going last. A day, a week, forever. I don't know. I'm not trying to hurt you."

"Then what the hell was that? Why didn't you just leave instead of holding me?"

"That was us grieving for our child." He leaned into her. "Something we should have done ten years ago. I'm not a heartless bastard, Lucy. I realize you went through hell, but that doesn't change things."

"Lane."

He crossed the living room and reached for the knob. "Goodbye, Lucy."

LANE SAT ON the picnic table outside the Airstream looking up at the stars.

"How could things have gone so wrong?" He'd thought he was on cloud nine when he woke up that morning. Lies punched you in the gut and anger propelled you past the pain. What he'd been feeling for the past few weeks hadn't been a lie. They had become a little family and he'd loved every second of it. He wanted to forgive Lucy, he truly did, but there were some things in life a man couldn't forgive. And the woman he loved marrying another man while carrying his child was one of them. Never mind that she'd kept their baby a secret. He didn't know if he had the strength to get past that.

He didn't even know where to begin. The last thing he wanted was to answer questions from his bunkmates. And his mother... Well, she had warned him. Tonight he didn't want to be around anyone. Lexi had offered the trailer after she'd dropped him off at his truck. She hadn't asked him any questions and he hadn't offered any explanations. He'd been friends with her and Shane for a long time and she'd assured him they wouldn't mind him camping out for a night.

He unlocked the vintage trailer door and flopped on the couch. He looked around; it was small, but it was private. "Maybe this is what I need." He'd seen horse trailer-RV combinations. "Just take off, do odd stable jobs around the country. Just me and my horses."

What about Carina?

How easily her little face came to mind. Tonight he'd promised never to abandon her and he intended on keeping that promise. It might not be easy; in fact, he knew it would be damn difficult. But over time, he'd think of Lucy less and less. It had been different before. He didn't know why she'd left then, and now he did. It made a world of difference.

It angered him to think about how Nicolino had treated him. If Nicolino had known she wasn't coming back when he left for Wyoming, he should have told him despite the questions Lane would have asked. He would've stayed out there. He never would've come back. *That's a lie.* He would've come back for his mother, for Curly, for Rusty. The entire time he'd been in Wyoming, he'd missed Ramblewood. It wasn't just because of Lucy.

It didn't matter anymore. It was over. Lane fluffed up one of the pillows on the couch and stretched out. He'd worry about it tomorrow. Tonight he didn't want to think about Lucy, Carina…or his son.

They'd had a son…

LANE WOKE TO the sound of pounding the next morning. He'd never been fond of waking up and not knowing where he was, and since Lucy had been back in town, it'd happened twice. His head throbbed in rhythm with the pounding. He climbed off the couch and swung open the door.

"It's about time you woke up." Rusty pushed past him. "I've been trying to call you all night."

"What for?" Lane grumbled. Shane had found his phone and given it to Lexi. After that he'd turned it off.

"Your mama and I are getting hitched." Rusty slapped him on the back. "I thought it only fitting that you be the first to know."

I need a drink. "Congratulations." Lane rummaged through the trailer until he found a bottle of whiskey. He pulled out two red plastic cups and set them on the counter. After pouring two fingers in each, he handed one to Rusty. "Here's to the happy couple." Lane tossed back his drink.

Rusty glanced around the trailer. "You here alone?"

"Sure am, and I intend on staying that way." Lane

poured himself another drink, screwed the cap back on the bottle and set it back in the cabinet. "I didn't think you would ever break your bachelor status." Lane tossed back another and slammed his empty cup on the counter. "You treat her good or else you'll have to answer to me. And don't expect me to call you Daddy."

"Heard you had some excitement with the little one last night." Rusty sat on the couch.

"That was bad enough. It was what happened afterward that blew me away."

Lane excused himself to the bathroom. When he came back out, Rusty had a serious expression plastered across his face.

"Seeing as we're going to be family and all, you should be able to talk to me about anything."

Lane laughed at the older man. "I've been coming to you with my problems since I was a kid. It's nothing new. I just choose not to discuss this one."

"Suit yourself. Just do me a favor this time. Leave my saddle out of it. The last time you were down in the dumps, you made it so slick I darn near killed myself," Rusty grumbled. "Now, how would you feel about being my best man?"

Lane joined him on the couch. "I'd be honored. You make my mom happy when you're not driving her crazy."

That silence he enjoyed with Lucy and Carina when they were riding home in his truck was perfect. The silence he was experiencing now with Rusty staring at him, waiting for him to explode, didn't quite have the same effect.

"If I tell you, you can't tell Mom. Our private conversations override any 'we tell each other everything' pacts you might have with her." The last thing he needed was his mom meddling in his business. He loved her dearly, but she didn't need to know every detail of his life. This was one of them.

"You have my word as a gentleman."

Coming from anybody else, that would be laughable, but coming from Rusty, it actually meant something.

"I found out why Lucy left me ten years ago."

Over the next three hours, he rehashed the entire series of events leading up to his sleeping in the Airstream.

"That's a tough one, son. I understand where you're both coming from."

"If she had married Antonio after the miscarriage, I think I would've understood." Lane knew he would have been able to forgive her. "But this man planned to raise my child and keep it from me. My child! You don't steal another man's baby. I don't care what I said back then about not having kids." Lane took a deep breath and exhaled slowly. "I take responsibility for my part in this. But that doesn't excuse what she did. It would have been one thing if I had been a violent man or her life had been in danger. I was a stupid kid who said he didn't want kids, and based on that, they were going to pass my child off as Antonio's. That's reprehensible."

"Do you love her?" Rusty asked.

"I'm not as sure of it as I was twenty-four hours ago." Lane had always thought of Lucy as the one great love who'd gotten away. None of the women he'd been with since had compared to her. Which seemed ridiculous now. He had compared grown women to a teenage infatuation. What he thought was love back then was probably more lust than anything. They'd been two kids with big plans. He'd be willing to bet 99 percent of kids at that age had similar plans.

"Sounds like you have some thinking to do." Rusty slapped him on the back.

"That's exactly what I don't need to be doing," Lane said. "What time is it, anyway?"

Rusty checked his watch. "It's almost ten o'clock."

Lane tugged on his boots. "How did you know I was here, anyway?"

"Shane told me."

"Well, that figures. Let's head out of here." Lane locked up the trailer and rehid the key. "I really am happy for you and Mom."

LUCY HOPED SHE wasn't calling Ella's house too early Sunday morning. She'd wanted to call last night but it had been too late. After three rings, Ella answered the phone, her voice slightly groggy.

"I didn't mean to wake you."

"Lucy, are you okay? Lexi called last night and told us about Carina. You were still at the hospital and she said you'd probably call once she'd been released.

When I hadn't heard from you, I assumed you went home and got some much-needed rest."

"Oh, Ella, it's awful. Between Carina's accident and Lane finding out everything, I don't know what to do."

"You're going to start by drying your eyes before that young'un of yours wakes up. I'll be right over." Ella hung up the phone before Lucy could argue.

Ten minutes later, Ella let herself in the front door and joined her at the kitchen table. "What happened? Start from the beginning and don't leave anything out."

Lucy proceeded to tell Ella about Carina's accident and everything that had happened once they'd arrived home.

"I think you need to take a moment to cool down. Carina's going to be just fine, and as for Lane, it was a lot for him to absorb at once." While she appreciated Ella's positive vibes, she believed the opposite. Lane was finished. "Have you tried calling him?"

"No." Lucy refused to be the woman who called and hounded a man who wanted nothing to do with her. A small part of her might have wanted to, but she was stronger than that; she was worth more than that. "My biggest concern is Carina. He promised not to disappear from her life, and I have to trust him."

"Lane's not going anywhere. He left that one time to go to Wyoming and it didn't work out. It wouldn't have worked out whether you were there with him or not. If he says he'll still be there for Carina, he will be. He's a man of his word."

"Fine, but how do I tell my daughter we'll never have another family outing?" As much as she appreciated everything Lane had done for Carina, she wished she'd never involved her daughter in any of it. She'd keep the next man in her life far away, if there was a next man. Lucy couldn't even imagine being with any man except Lane. And now he was gone.

"You don't." Ella placed her hands over Lucy's. "This is not like Antonio. You have tomorrow. You have the next day. You told him the truth and that's the best thing you could've done. You both need time to process everything. It's not a race to the finish line. Enjoy your time alone with Carina, because before you know it, she'll be going off to college. I don't have that luxury. When you have five kids, you very rarely get to spend time alone with one. Use this time to your advantage."

Lucy hadn't looked at it that way. She'd always felt bad Carina had been an only child. She'd never considered how special their relationship was compared to larger families. But she'd had a taste of family life with Lane and she wasn't ready to give up that dream, not yet.

"How's Carina feeling?" Lexi greeted her Monday morning outside the lab door.

"Good enough to go to school." Lucy sighed when she didn't see any sign of Lane. It had been more wishful thinking than anything. He'd said he needed space, and she'd give it to him.

"And Lane?" she asked. "He didn't say anything,

but he looked pretty rough when I picked him up." Lexi unlocked the door and held it open for Lucy to enter. "I'm not going to stick my nose in your business, but if you're fighting about Carina's accident—"

"We're not. We're fighting over something that happened ten years ago."

Lexi laughed. "I could write a whole book on that subject."

One of the biggest differences between barn management and breed management was the abundance of female companionship. It was impossible to feel bad about a situation when you had an entire team of women cheering you on. They might not know all the specifics, but they had your back.

"So now we're giving each other space, and it's Carina's birthday in a few days. I don't know if I should invite him or not. It's just a small family gathering. You and Shane are welcome to come. I don't want to crowd him, but I don't want to disappoint my daughter, either."

"I'd ask him. It's not for your benefit—it's for Carina's," Lexi said. "You know how men can be, so definitely preface the invitation with the fact that you're asking for Carina and keep any reference to you two out of it. I think he'll understand. Better yet, call him on the phone. Call him now so I can pinch you if you say too much."

Lucy took a few deep breaths before she dialed Lane's cell phone number. He answered on the first ring.

"Hello."

Okay, the fact that he'd answered her call was a start. "Hi. I wanted to let you know we're having a small birthday party for Carina on Thursday night at the house. It's for family, but I know she would love to see you there. There's nothing more to it than that."

"Of course I'll be there," Lane said. For a moment, it sounded as if he wanted to say more, but he didn't.

"Great. We'll see you then. Have a good day." Lexi motioned for her to hang up the phone.

"See, you did it." Lexi patted her on the back. "Let's go check on our foals. You look like you could use a dose of cuteness right about now."

Lucy followed Lexi out of the lab a little more hopeful that she had been a few minutes earlier. Her daughter deserved an amazing birthday. It was the first one she'd celebrate without Antonio and Lucy didn't want anything to spoil it. Carina didn't need to know Lucy and Lane had broken up until after her birthday. Every child deserved a special day of happiness.

Chapter Thirteen

"Make a wish." Lucy held Carina's hair out of the way as she blew out her candles. "And don't tell anyone your wish or else it won't come true."

"That's a cute cake," Lane said to Nicolino. It was two tiers of bubblegum pink with silver horseshoes and other tack around the sides. A giant American paint horse closely resembling Jigsaw sat lounging on top.

"Ella had Maggie Dalton custom-make it for Carina, but after the accident, she was a little nervous about picking it up."

"Did you ever think we would be standing around a nine-year-old girl's birthday party discussing cake?"

"Especially pink cake," Nicolino added. "I hear Jigsaw is doing really well."

"Funny thing… Lexi told me all the vet bills had been paid in advance. Would you happen to know something about that?"

"Me?" Nicolino feigned surprise. "I have no idea what you are talking about. I think I hear Ella calling me."

Lane laughed. He knew enough not to push the issue. Some people's actions spoke louder than words.

For a kid who had taken the ride of her life less than a week ago, Carina looked remarkably well. He'd sat up thinking about her and Lucy almost every night since then. Two months ago, he hadn't even known Carina existed; now his life wouldn't be complete without her in it. And as much as he had tried to convince himself Lucy had been nothing more than a teenage infatuation, it didn't explain how he felt this time around. He'd asked her for space and she'd given it to him. After searching his heart, he felt strong enough to give their relationship another chance. That is, if Lucy was still open to the idea.

"I have a little something for you." He sat next to Carina on the couch and handed her a pink-and-silver gift bag.

Carina removed the tissue paper and peered into it. "Mamma, look!" She pulled out a turquoise T-shirt and held it up in front of her.

"What does it say on the front?" Lucy leaned in for a closer look. "'World's Bravest Cowgirl.'"

"Thank you." Carina wrapped her good arm around his neck and gave him a kiss on the cheek. "I love it."

Lane had never picked out clothing for anyone other than himself before. He'd been nervous about the color and size. He guessed it had been good practice for when he had kids someday. Hopefully, that day would come sooner rather than later.

"You look deep in thought." Lucy handed him a glass of wine.

"Thank you. I was just thinking about you." Lane gestured to the front door.

Lucy nodded and followed him onto the porch. "Do I dare ask what you were thinking about me?

"I know we haven't been around each other much as adults." Lane sat in the same rocking chair he had that first night. "But I think we're mature enough to know who we like and what we like. I feel different when I'm around you."

Lucy sat next to him in the other chair. "How do you feel?"

"Complete." Lane couldn't believe he was about to put his heart on the line. "You know my history. My parents never formed the perfect family unit. I don't have one picture of my mom, my dad and me together, so believe me when I say the concept is very foreign to me. But when I'm with you and Carina, it feels natural. It feels right, like this is what it's all about."

"Do you still feel that way?" Lucy asked. "Can you look at me and honestly say you feel more love than hurt where I'm concerned?"

"I've always loved you, Lucy." Lane reached for her hand. "Even when I was mad at you. Even when you married somebody else, I still loved you. I may have hated what happened between us, but I never stopped loving you."

"Is it enough?" Lucy asked. "Is your love enough to overcome the past? Because admittedly, I've been the offender. Is there enough love to forgive the things I've done?"

Lane knew in his heart that he'd been partially to blame. "I'm the one who asked you to leave your family and everything you knew in Italy and in Texas to move to a state you had never seen, never even really heard of…and then I had the nerve to be surprised when you never showed. Honestly, who could blame you?" He hadn't realized how presumptuous he'd been until he'd said the words aloud. "I think the question you should be asking is if you can forgive yourself. You've carried all this guilt for things that were out of your control. You can speculate about our baby all you want, and you're never going to have an answer. But I am glad you told me. And yes, I've thought—a lot. I think we not only have enough love, we have a love strong enough to survive."

"Where do we go from here?" Lucy asked.

"I know where I would like to go." Lane stood, holding her hand in his. Then he knelt before her on one knee. "I'd like to take this to the next level and share a life with you, the life we—"

"The life we missed out on?"

Lane shook his head. "We didn't miss out on anything. We were a little sidetracked. That doesn't mean it's too late."

"What are you asking me?"

"I don't have some big speech prepared and I don't have a diamond ring. I can buy you a diamond ring and I can write you a speech someday, but all I can offer you right now is a promise. A promise to love you, a promise to always be by your side and a promise to make you my wife, if you'll have me."

"Yes! I would love to be your wife."

"That was it! My wish!" Carina shouted from inside the cottage. The front door flew open and she ran onto the porch. "My wish came true!"

Lane straightened and pulled Lucy to her feet. Somehow he had the feeling many more intimate moments like this would be interrupted in their future together. But he didn't care.

"How long have you been listening at the window?" Lucy asked.

"I wasn't listening. I was watching." Carina giggled. "I wanted to put my presents on the table by the window and that's when I saw you kneeling in front of Mamma." Carina turned to Lane. "You did ask her, right?"

"Yes." Lane couldn't believe she'd wished her mother would marry him. Lane sat in the rocking chair so he'd be eye level with her. "Carina, are you sure you're okay with this?"

Carina nodded eagerly. "I've never been more ready. You love Mamma and she loves you. What more is there?"

"You look beautiful, Mamma."

"You're the most gorgeous bride I've ever seen." Ella finished fastening the back of Lucy's vintage-inspired ivory-lace-and-organza wedding gown. She hadn't had one when she'd married Antonio and still couldn't believe she was wearing one now. She needed someone to pinch her so she'd finally believe her wedding day to Lane was here.

Lucy braved a look in the mirror. The dress was stunning. It was the first one she'd seen and she'd fallen in love with its lace straps, sweetheart neckline and lace racer back instantly. Having been married and divorced, she hadn't even planned on a wedding gown, but Ella had insisted. And she was glad she'd listened.

"Are you ready for me to walk you down the aisle?" Nicolino peeked his head in the door. *"Che bellissima!"* Tears formed in his eyes.

"Grazie." Lucy promised herself she wouldn't cry and ruin her makeup. "Don't you start, because once you start, then I will."

It was Christmas Eve. Lucy and Lane stood in the middle of Ella and Nicolino's living room as their closest friends and family formed a circle around them. The groom had never looked more charming in his jet-black tuxedo.

"I hope to heavens this is legal." Rusty cleared his throat and joined the couple's hands together. Lucy and Lane had both agreed he was the perfect person to officiate their wedding. Now that he was ordained, he wanted everyone to call him Preacher Rusty. "Ladies and gentlemen, we are gathered here today to join this lovesick cowboy with his Italian cowgirl once and for all."

The room erupted in laughter. "In all seriousness... I've been on this earth for seventy-five years and I've never seen a couple more made for each other than these two. Although my sweetheart, Barbara, and I come in a close second. Most of the people in this room watched these two kids fall in love with each other way back when they were teenagers. It's about time they tied the knot."

"Lucille Giovanna Travisonno, do you take this man to be your beloved husband, in sickness and in health, for better or for worse, in horse hair and mud, forsaking all others for as long as you both shall live?"

"I do." Lucy wanted to laugh. She wanted to cry. But smiling won out when she looked into Lane's eyes. They were doing this… They were really getting married.

"And do you, Lane Foster Morgan, take this magnificent woman to be your beloved wife, in sickness and in health, for better or for worse, in Italian or English, forsaking all others for as long as you both shall live?"

"I do."

"Little miss." Rusty nodded to Carina. "Come on up here, sweetie."

Her daughter was beautiful in her tea-length pale ivory dress. Carina placed her left hand on top of Lane's and Lucy's.

"Do you, Miss Carina, bless this marriage between your mother and Lane?"

"I do." Carina smiled at both of them. Tears began to well in her eyes.

"Rusty, you better marry us before I start to cry," Lucy warned.

"Miss Carina, do you have the rings?"

Carina removed two gold bands from the satin drawstring bag tied around her wrist and handed them to Rusty.

"These rings are a symbol of your love and commitment to each another, forming an unbroken circle. Lane, place this ring on Lucy's finger and repeat after me."

Lane's steady hands clasped hers. "I got this part." She gazed into his eyes as he slid the ring on her finger, her heart finally calm after ten years. "With this ring, I thee wed."

Lucy didn't think she could smile any bigger without bursting.

Lucy slid Lane's ring on his finger, her voice caught in her throat. This was it. This was their moment. "With this ring, I thee wed."

"By the power granted to me, I now pronounce these two hitched! You may kiss the bride."

Lane placed his hands on both sides of her face and kissed her mouth sweetly. "I love you, Lucy, for all eternity."

Everyone in the room began to clap.

"We have one more ceremony to perform," Rusty said.

Lane removed a red velvet box from his jacket pocket and knelt on one knee in front of Carina. He opened the box and removed a silver bangle bracelet.

"Carina, this bracelet symbolizes my love for you. Never ending, never broken. I will always be there for you, whether it's today, tomorrow or on your wedding day."

Lucy's hand flew to her chest. She hadn't known Lane had planned such a touching gesture to include Carina in the ceremony.

He slipped the bangle onto her wrist and took her hand in his. "I love you, munchkin."

Carina threw her arms around his neck. "I love you, too."

"Now, if you three will join hands in the middle, everyone will join hands around you." Rusty looked around the room, satisfied. "On this day, in front of family and friends and the Almighty above, I now pronounce you a family."

* * * * *

REQUEST YOUR FREE BOOKS!
2 FREE NOVELS PLUS 2 FREE GIFTS!

H HARLEQUIN®

American Romance®

LOVE, HOME & HAPPINESS

YES! Please send me 2 FREE Harlequin® American Romance® novels and my 2 FREE gifts (gifts are worth about $10). After receiving them, if I don't wish to receive any more books, I can return the shipping statement marked "cancel." If I don't cancel, I will receive 4 brand-new novels every month and be billed just $4.74 per book in the U.S. or $5.49 per book in Canada. That's a savings of at least 12% off the cover price! It's quite a bargain! Shipping and handling is just 50¢ per book in the U.S. and 75¢ per book in Canada.* I understand that accepting the 2 free books and gifts places me under no obligation to buy anything. I can always return a shipment and cancel at any time. Even if I never buy another book, the two free books and gifts are mine to keep forever.

154/354 HDN GHZZ

Name	(PLEASE PRINT)

Address	Apt. #

City	State/Prov.	Zip/Postal Code

Signature (if under 18, a parent or guardian must sign)

Mail to the **Reader Service:**
IN U.S.A.: P.O. Box 1867, Buffalo, NY 14240-1867
IN CANADA: P.O. Box 609, Fort Erie, Ontario L2A 5X3

Want to try two free books from another line?
Call 1-800-873-8635 or visit www.ReaderService.com.

* Terms and prices subject to change without notice. Prices do not include applicable taxes. Sales tax applicable in N.Y. Canadian residents will be charged applicable taxes. Offer not valid in Quebec. This offer is limited to one order per household. Not valid for current subscribers to Harlequin American Romance books. All orders subject to credit approval. Credit or debit balances in a customer's account(s) may be offset by any other outstanding balance owed by or to the customer. Please allow 4 to 6 weeks for delivery. Offer available while quantities last.

Your Privacy—The Reader Service is committed to protecting your privacy. Our Privacy Policy is available online at www.ReaderService.com or upon request from the Reader Service.

We make a portion of our mailing list available to reputable third parties that offer products we believe may interest you. If you prefer that we not exchange your name with third parties, or if you wish to clarify or modify your communication preferences, please visit us at www.ReaderService.com/consumerchoice or write to us at Reader Service Preference Service, P.O. Box 9062, Buffalo, NY 14240-9062. Include your complete name and address.

HARI5

ℐAmerican ℛomance®

Garrett Lockhart has no idea the woman he's about to meet is someone he's about to get to know very well! The sexy military doctor is immediately entranced by Hope Winslow…and her darling baby son.

Read on for a sneak peek at
A TEXAS SOLDIER'S FAMILY
from Cathy Gillen Thacker's new
TEXAS LEGACIES: THE LOCKHARTS miniseries!

"Welcome aboard!" The flight attendant smiled. "Going home to Texas…?"

"Not voluntarily," Garrett Lockhart muttered under his breath.

It wasn't that he didn't *appreciate* spending time with his family. He did. It's just that he didn't want them weighing in on what his next step should be.

Reenlist and take the considerable promotion being offered?

Or take a civilian post that would allow him to pursue his dreams?

He had twenty-nine days to decide and an unspecified but pressing family crisis to handle in the meantime.

And an expensive-looking blonde in a white power suit who'd been sizing him up from a distance, ever since he arrived at the gate…

He'd noticed her, too. Hard not to with that gorgeous face, mane of long, silky hair brushing against her shoulders, and a smoking-hot body.

Phone to her ear, one hand trying to retract the telescoping handle of her suitcase while still managing the carryall over her shoulder, she said, "Have to go…Yes, yes. I'll call you as soon as I land in Dallas. Not to worry." She laughed softly, charmingly, while lifting her suitcase with one hand into the overhead compartment. "If you-all will just *wait* until I can—*ouch!*" He heard her stumble toward him, yelping as her expensive leather carryall crashed onto his lap.

"Let me help you," he drawled. With one hand hooked around her waist and the other around her shoulders, he lifted her quickly and skillfully to her feet, then turned and lowered her so she landed squarely in her own seat. That done, he handed her the carryall she'd inadvertently assaulted him with.

Hope knew she should say something. If only to make her later job easier.

And she would have, if the sea blue eyes she'd been staring into hadn't been so mesmerizing. She liked his hair, too. So dark and thick and…touchable…

"Ma'am?" he prodded again, less patiently.

Clearly he was expecting some response to ease the unabashed sexual tension that had sprung up between them, so she said the first thing that came into her mind. "Thank you for your assistance just now. And for your service. To our country, I mean."

His dark brow furrowed. His lips—so firm and sensual—thinned. Shoulders flexing, he studied her with breathtaking intent, then asked, "How'd you know I was in the military?"

Don't miss
A TEXAS SOLDIER'S FAMILY
by Cathy Gillen Thacker, available July 2016
everywhere Harlequin® Western Romance®
books and ebooks are sold.

www.Harlequin.com

Same great stories, new name!

In July 2016,
the HARLEQUIN®
AMERICAN ROMANCE® series
will become
the HARLEQUIN®
WESTERN ROMANCE series.

Connect with us to find your next great read,
special offers and more.

/HarlequinBooks

@HarlequinBooks

www.HarlequinBlog.com

www.Harlequin.com/Newsletters

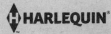

HARLEQUIN®

A *Romance* FOR EVERY MOOD™

www.Harlequin.com

HWR2016